Escaping 1

Journey out of trauma back to love and safety

Copyright 2022
Chistell Publishing
https://www.chistell.com
First Printing, January 2022

Published by: Chistell Publishing
                   7235 Aventine Way, Suite #201
                   Chattanooga, TN 37421

Author: Denise Turney

                   ISBN: 9780578230344

Dedication

For my son.

I love you, Gregory –

Chapter One

A northern cardinal, its red crest flattened by the whip of high winds, slammed into Clarissa Maxwell's large, bay window. Oak and birch leaves, muddled together with broken tree branches, were strewn across the front and back yards, remaining evidence of last night's storm, a noisy event that had brought pounding rains and shaken Clarissa out of sleep.

Sitting in an upholstered chair across from the bay window, Clarissa, a thirty-eight-year-old single woman who'd moved to Georgia several years ago after vacationing in the state, looked down at her laptop screen and frowned. Her brow tightened into ugly lines. Pulling the ends of her cornrows behind her ears, she fell back against her dining room chair. "Damn," she cursed to the spacious dining room in her luxury two-story Sandy Springs, Georgia townhouse. "Two years and I still haven't published a new novel. I can't go deeper into debt," she scowled. "I'm almost buried."

Money woes were pushing her close to anxiety. She almost sighed when she heard Mary Newton's song "Who's To Blame" sound across her cell phone, demanding her attention. Normally, she left the phone on mute, especially while she was working. But, she'd turned the ringer on this morning after receiving a text from her sister, April.

She was upbeat as she sang, "Hey, April. What's up?" into the phone.

"Job stress," April laughed.

"You or me?" Clarissa asked, staring at her laptop's empty screen.

"I was talking about me," April said. "These six senior managers who I support are about to drive me nuts. They are so demanding," she moaned. "I'm starting to feel like I can't do this job anymore." After a pause, she lowered her voice and added, "I don't want to fail."

The sisters, their bond strong since childhood, talked for twenty minutes, interrupting their upsets with laughter every few minutes. Finally, April said, "Let me get off this phone. I've got a butt-kicking project to knock out before morning. But first, I've got to get dinner on the table."

"What's for dinner?" Clarissa asked.

"Spaghetti and homemade tomato sauce."

"Send me some," Clarissa begged. "Love your homemade tomato sauce."

"Love you more than anything," April chuckled.

"You're the best sister ever," Clarissa avowed.

"Well, Sister, treat me to your new novel."

"I'm telling you, April," Clarissa began, glancing toward the bay window. "If I don't get a new novel written soon, I'm going to be out of my home." She paused. "It's probably why I've been feeling out-of-sorts." She shook her head. "I gotta find something to write a novel about. I have to," she added, more volume in her voice. "It's mid-July, the time when I've usually been working on a good story. But, not this year," she sighed. "Something's wrong."

"Call me if you want to talk about it," April offered.

"I will," Clarissa nodded, chewing her bottom lip.

****

Two weeks later, Clarissa stared at her blank laptop screen. "That's it," she stood and moaned.

Before she knew it, she was searching the Internet for cabins to rent in northern Georgia. She'd stayed in the area twice. The first time she stayed in the area was two years ago. The second time was last summer.

Northern Georgia offered peace, rolling hills, wild flowers, creeks and the nearby Chattahoochee River, shutting out the world's noise. She'd written her eleventh novel two years ago while renting a cabin in those hills. The book, a science fiction romance, had turned out to be her best selling novel to date, landing on the *Essence, USA Today, Publisher's Weekly* and the *New York Times* bestseller lists.

An hour later, Clarissa printed the email receipt that she'd received from Mozark Cabins Travel Services. Then, she shut down her laptop, packed it in its leather carry case and placed the case atop her large, wheeled soft-side suitcase. The suitcase was stuffed with enough clothes for her to wear for a month.

That night while she slept in her Sandy Springs townhouse, it wasn't a fierce, unrelenting storm that pulled Clarissa away from sleep. Instead, it was nightmares, dreadful dreams that promised regret. The dreams were so terrifying that Clarissa had shaken herself awoke with the sound of her own piercing screams. Her heart had been racing and her chest felt tight. As she'd wiped sweat from her face, neck and arms, she had kept telling herself that the nightmares were a product of her money worries. But, she didn't believe it. The nightmares had been like visions, filled with haunting clarity.

While she washed her face in her primary bathroom the following morning, she told herself to focus on the sound of the water rushing out of the sink spigot, anything to steer her thoughts away from the faces that she'd seen in her nightmares. "I'm just worried about staying away from the city for so long," she tried, as she dabbed her face dry.

She dressed hurriedly. Then, she packed and toted her luggage, her handgun and book bag downstairs into the living room. Luggage in the living room, she entered the kitchen where she scrambled and ate three eggs for breakfast, took her vitamins and drank a glass of cranberry juice. After she washed the dishes, she went into the first floor guest bathroom and peed.

A moment later, she hurried into the living room and placed her Glock handgun in its case. After she put the gun case in her book bag, she glanced over her shoulder, checking to see if she'd forgotten anything. Certain that she hadn't, she headed outside, locked her townhouse and walked toward her burgundy Toyota Camry, silently praying to God for writing inspiration.

****

Yellow daffodils, pink, red and purple tulips and blue irises sprang up on the sides of the narrow, two lane highway that Clarissa drove down for miles. Flowers, nature, color -- they were what Clarissa loved about the hills of North Georgia, especially the area surrounding the Mozark Cabins. She hadn't seen nature explode with so much color since she'd visited the cabins a year ago. The hills rolled with green grass, plants and trees that birds and squirrel played in, their chirps and squeaks going up like an exuberant chorus.

The Camry's dashboard recorded an outside temperature of ninety-four degrees. Yet, Clarissa punched the window remote and rolled her driver side window down, letting cold air escape. Less than a quarter mile ahead, on the right side of the road, was a creek. Thanks to the previous night's pouring rain, Clarissa was confident that the creek running behind the Mozark Cabins was full, allowing her to hear the creek gurgle, even if only faintly.

Swinging around a curve in the highway, she turned the car radio off and listened. Although sound of the creek flowing escaped her, she smiled when she heard birds playing in the trees, reminding her of how nature remained untouched by commercialism out here.

Nature's tranquility continued to relax her as she drove around another curve, then looked up and saw a familiar red, brick building. A wooden sign with "Mozark Cabins Travel Services" printed in thick black letters across its front was placed in the building's front window.

Clarissa pulled inside the travel services' driveway. She left her luggage inside her car and headed for the building's entrance.

"I was waiting for you," a red-haired woman with a tall, slender build stood and smiled. She walked toward Clarissa with her hand extended. "My name is Sandy. You're Clarissa, right?"

"Yes," Clarissa nodded. "Stopping by to get the key to the cabin that I'm renting."

"Certainly," Sandy responded.

"Can I have the same cabin that I rented last year?" Clarissa asked. "I feel inspired to create while I'm there. I didn't write a new novel at the cabin last year. Instead, I wrote several short stories that I published in a few magazines." She smiled. "But, short stories don't yield enough money to live on." Glancing over Sandy's head, she added, "This time, I have to write a full-length novel." She sighed. "Right now, I need all the help that I can get to sit down and knock out a good story."

"You're in luck," Sandy said. "The cabin that you want is our last vacancy this month. That's how I knew it was you when you walked through the door. We received your payment yesterday, and you've already completed and signed all of the paperwork online."

Clarissa waited while Sandy walked behind her desk and searched through a metal filing cabinet.

"We're leaving for several weeks tomorrow," Sandy revealed. "You rented right on time."

"Going anywhere special?" Clarissa asked. "And how long will your office be closed?"

"We're a small, family-owned travel company. It's just me and my sister. We're headed for Hawaii for two weeks. After that, we're going to Miami for a week."

"Those are great vacation spots," Clarissa said. "Your sister said she loved tropical climate. She's real nice."

"Thank you," Sandy smiled. "If you need anything urgent while we're away, call the authorities. Someone can help you. Plus, the cabin that you like so much is next to a cabin a wonderful couple owns."

"They are wonderful," Clarissa said, recalling the husband and wife couple from the two previous times when she'd rented the cabin. "And, don't worry about me," she waved as she took the key from Sandy. "I was in the military. I know how to take care of myself. On top of that, this is a very safe area. I've lived in some tough places. I know how to handle myself in nearly any situation," she nodded. "Compared to other places I've been to, this place is like heaven. I really do love it out here."

"Well, we hope that you keep coming back."

"Thank you," Clarissa nodded. "Enjoy your vacation."

"We will," Sandy smiled. She walked Clarissa to the office door. "Oh, and, if there's anything in the cabin basement, just leave it," she said. "Like you, the previous occupants are regulars, except they stay at the cabin three to four months a year. We told them that they could store non-valuables in the basement, they stay at that particular cabin so often. And, like I said," she added. "We're a small, family-owned company. We love taking care of our clients."

"That's what I love about working with you," Clarissa told her. She pushed the office door open and headed outside. "You take such good care of the people who do business with you."

After she slid across the driver seat, she looked up and waved to Sandy. Then, she put her car in reverse and backed out of the driveway.

Five miles later, passing rows of red maple, pine, oak and sycamore trees, she had only seen seven cabins. She glanced through the windshield, fixing her gaze on the winding highway, as countryside stretched out before her like miles of green carpet. Half a mile ahead was a truck stop and a small sit-down restaurant that served the best greasy food any hungry trucker would want to eat. At the truck stop were also six gasoline pumps and a convenience store that looked like it hadn't been cleaned in months. The far end of the convenience store housed four showers and two overnight sleeping rooms.

Clarissa barely looked at the large truck stop, a dozen cars and twice as many class eight cargo trucks filling the gravel parking lot. Across the highway from the truck stop was the Chattahoochee River. To Clarissa, the truck stop, although necessary, was an eyesore, distracting from the beauty in the area. Before she knew it, she'd pressed her foot on the accelerator, sending the Camry speeding down the highway more than fifteen miles over the posted speed limit of sixty miles an hour.

"There it is," Clarissa smiled, lowering her head and looking out of the passenger window. At the peak of a grassy hill was a four-story, cherry wood log cabin, a green gabled metal roof crowning three raked windows on the house's top floor.

Clarissa slowed the Camry to a crawl. Even before she pulled into the driveway, images of the cabin's finished attic, a queen sized bed with soft goose feather down pillows, a writing desk and two metal file cabinets, flashed across her mind. Then, there was the writing room across the hall from the primary bedroom, a massive room with a three-seat sofa, two ebony wood dressers, a six-foot floor mirror trimmed in gold, a walk-in closet and an en suite with a garden bathtub.

Yet, as much as Clarissa loved the writing room across the hall from the primary bedroom and the writing desk in the attic, it was the living room writing desk that attracted her most. That writing desk, a hand carved roll-top desk, overlooked a set of custom picture windows, inviting in enough sun rays to keep Clarissa's spirit and energy up. It was through the windows that Clarissa could easily detect the smell of purple and pink azaleas and rhododendrons. All she had to do was to push the windows open and the flowers would fill the living room with the sweetest, soft scents.

The first thing that Clarissa did when she pulled up to the side of the cabin was to pop open the Camry's trunk and grab her suitcase, book bag and laptop. Then, she headed up the side walkway.

The cabin's interior was as it had been when she'd stayed in it a year ago. "Well," she mused, eyeballing the living room, dining room and kitchen. "It's time to start working on a great, new novel."

She spent that first day indoors, except for the half hour that she'd swept leaves off the front and back porches and stopped by a small grocery store seven miles north of her cabin. She refused to let herself consider that she'd spent two thousand dollars to rent the cabin, and this at a time when she only had eight thousand dollars left in her bank account and no source of income outside of her writing and dwindling book sales.

Despite her best intentions, Clarissa didn't even open the living room's roll-top writing desk. Instead, she popped a large bowl of popcorn, layered the popcorn with melted margarine and, plopping down on the living room sofa, watched three movies on Fenzi and one movie on Tuvi. The movies didn't inspire her to write. Yet, she'd found them entertaining, especially *Crimson Tide*, the Navy flick starring Denzel Washington and Gene Hackman. The movies also didn't shake the gnawing depression that was starting to jab at her. She was yet to connect the rhododendrons outside the cabin window with the flowers in her nightmares.

Chapter Two

The next morning, Clarissa tossed her book bag across her shoulders and went for a brisk six mile run along the dirt road in front of her cabin, loose soil flying up each time the heels of her sneakers hit the ground. Half a mile away from the end of the dirt road was the two lane highway that Clarissa had driven to the cabin on. Her stride was open, fluid while she ran, bringing her a deep satisfaction.

Her run back to the cabin was also smooth. Yet, the run demanded more of her lungs, forced her to take in deeper breaths. She ran with intent, her knees rising to her abdomen, her arms moving with strength. The run felt sweet to Clarissa. She smiled when she spotted her cabin less than a quarter mile ahead.

Five yards from the cabin, her mood shifted. She approached the flowers at the cabin's edge. That's when she noticed it, a crack in the basement window. Even from where she stood, she saw that the crack was too large for hail or even an average sized rock to have created it. To her, it looked like someone had tried to break the window with their fist and enter the cabin.

She inched toward the window, kneeled, her right knee poking grass and dirt, and pulled her gun out of the book bag. She scanned the basement, shifting her body from one side of the broken window to the other.

Standing, she entered the cabin through the back door. After she locked the door, she tiptoed through the kitchen and headed down the basement steps. Her Navy training revealed itself as she turned the basement's three corners sharp and clean, the Glock pulled up in front of her chest, the trigger, pin and drop safeties off.

Two minutes later, she convinced herself that the basement was empty. She climbed the steps, reapplied her gun's safety mechanisms and returned the gun to its case and her book bag. Still, worry stabbed her thoughts. At the same time, she reminded herself of how safe the area was, how safe the area had always been.

To quiet the worry, she drove to a small hardware store at the edge of the Mozark Cabins community and bought nails, plywood, masking tape, two security cameras and heavy plastic. She nailed and taped the plastic and plywood to the basement window before she climbed the stairs and sat down to write.

Begging the muse to come, the same muse that had allowed her to write a bestseller two years ago, she opened the picture windows, plugged in her laptop and sat at the writing desk for two hours. At the end of those two hours, she hadn't so much as typed a paragraph.

That's when she started her search for ways to move beyond writer's block. Over the next couple of weeks, she tried painting, sightseeing, talking with April twice a week, singing out loud and cooking homemade meals. Nothing worked.

"The last thing that I need to do is to throw away five hundred dollars a week on a cabin out in the middle of a very beautiful nowhere," Clarissa told April two Sundays after she'd arrived at the cabin.

"You'll get that writing inspiration," April promised. "The muse will come, maybe today, maybe tomorrow. Trust God."

"I hope you're right," Clarissa sighed. "I'm getting desperate." She didn't tell April that she was planning on forgoing paying her mortgage if her situation didn't improve over the next three months.

The following morning, Clarissa got up earlier than she'd done since she'd arrived at the cabin. In fact, the sky was reddish orange when she threw back the comforter in the cabin's primary bedroom and headed for the bathroom to wash up.

She pulled on a pair of shorts, a t-shirt and her running shoes. Then, she trotted down the cabin stairs.

Temperatures were already hot. Humidity caused her to break out in a sweat before she ran a mile down the narrow dirt road. The sweet aroma shooting off the honeysuckle at the side of the road left a lingering scent. In long intervals, a mild breeze blew off the trees that bordered the road and kissed the sides of Clarissa's face. When Clarissa turned and looked toward the highway below, she spotted a dirty white van ambling down the highway, barely hitting twenty-five miles an hour.

The van, a bent Texas license plate screwed above its rear bumper, looked out of place to Clarissa. On top of that, the crack in her basement window flashed across her mind.

Her run slowed to a jog. Her legs felt heavy, weary with worry. A half mile later, she turned and raced back to her cabin.

Seeing no footprints in the grass at the front of her cabin, she ran onto the porch, jammed her key in the lock and pushed the door open. She checked the entire upstairs. Then, returning to the first floor, she checked the kitchen and, later, the basement. Her shoulders didn't lower until she returned to the kitchen, where she stood staring at the ceiling, working to calm her nerves.

She closed her eyes, let out a deep breath and walked to the refrigerator next to the back door, pouring herself a glass of water. She'd just returned the water pitcher to the refrigerator's second shelf when she heard a noise, footsteps landing with a soft thud at the back of the cabin. Laying the glass of water on the table, she parted the back door curtains and peered out, giving the two acre backyard sweeping glances.

Seeing nothing, she unlocked the door and walked onto the back porch. This time, she didn't hear anything. Still, she stood on the porch for several minutes, looking out over the yard, before she returned to the kitchen and locked the door.

The morning run having left her throat dry, she drank the rest of the water. Then, giving the back yard one last check, she walked into the living room and climbed the stairs.

"It's nothing," she told herself as she headed upstairs. "Probably just small animals playing in the back yard creating the noise I heard earlier. Plus, all my worry about writing a novel has me so stressed that I'm getting edgy, jumpy. I have to let this stress go before I start to see everything as a threat."

The air on the second floor was cool, inviting. Although the coolness didn't evaporate Clarissa's safety concerns, it did help to nudge her focus toward novel writing.

She enjoyed a brisk shower. Instead of lathering up the gold bar of soap in her wash rag, she layered her skin with a fresh rain scented body wash. Her hands went across her body in circular motions, turning the body wash into small bubbles. Water from the shower head splashed her shoulders, back and legs, rinsing away the body wash but not its sweet scent. The water, its predictable sound tapping the shower walls, relaxed her. She turned and appreciated the cool feel of the water as it cascaded down her face, neck, breasts and stomach. After she finished showering, she pulled on a pair of jean shorts, a t-shirt, ankle socks and sneakers.

Her stomach growling, she left the second floor and returned to the kitchen. She swung the refrigerator door open, pulled out a jug of grape juice and an assortment of vegetables. Then, she crossed the floor and grabbed a salad bowl and a bottle of balsamic vinegar salad dressing out of the cupboard.

Pulling a long, sharp knife out of the silverware drawer, she started slicing a tomato on the counter cutting board. In between slicing the tomato, she drank grape juice straight out of the jug.

She was alone in the cabin. There was no one else to consider, one of the things that she loved about living alone.

Juice jug on the counter, she picked a cucumber and a butternut squash off the cutting board and started slicing. The cucumber and butternut squash were sliced and tossed in the salad bowl with kale, the tomato and balsamic vinegar dressing when she heard a loud thump against the cabin's back door.

She froze, salad bowl in hand. Yet, all that she heard were chirping birds.

"It's nothing," Clarissa told herself, leaving the kitchen and entering the dining room. She sat at the dining room table across from a long picture window eating the salad and drinking grape juice. Out of the corners of her eyes, she spotted a blue jay and a northern mockingbird fly across the sky. Last year, when she visited the cabin, she'd spotted more than ten different types of birds. She chuckled and told herself that nature loved the area as much as she did.

Ten minutes later, she was back in the kitchen standing in front of the sink washing the bowl, fork and knife. Dishes washed, she lifted the grape juice jug off the counter and returned it to the refrigerator.

That's when she heard it again, a thump followed by the thud of footsteps. She froze. She listened, wondering if the noise was coming from the porch.

The thuds grew louder, came faster. Pressing her ear to the door, she knew that whatever was creating the noise sounded large enough to be a bear cub. Yet, she couldn't get the van out of her thoughts and she knew that the broken basement window had not been caused by a bear cub.

She didn't wait.

She ran through the dining room, into the living room and up the stairs. Her heart didn't stop racing until she yanked her gun out of her book bag. She thought about calling her sister, April, but decided against it, certain that she didn't have time to make a phone call.

Hurrying down the stairs, she ran to the back door. This time, when she looked through the door window, she swore that she saw what looked like a girl crouching next to her Camry that was parked at the edge of the back yard.

From where she stood looking out the window, the girl looked unkempt and lost. Her curled back, the way that she folded her arms across her chest, as if protecting something delicate and valuable, revealed that she was hiding. Even from inside the cabin, Clarissa noticed that the girl was shaking. She looked sleight of build, like a petite kid in her early teens.

Knowing what it felt like to feel frightened, Clarissa pulled up on her gun. Then, she opened the back door. Before she went to her car, she checked the other side of the cabin.

The area was clear.

Taking short, careful steps, Clarissa approached her car. From the way that the girl was shaking, she knew that the girl was alone. She wondered if the girl lived in the area.

The girl hid behind the Camry with her arms wrapped around her torso. She was peering at the ground and trembling uncontrollably.

"I'm not going to hurt you," Clarissa said, extending her hand. Even as she reached for the girl, Clarissa scanned the area, looking toward the front then the back of the cabin.

The girl recoiled and leaned back, closer to the Camry. Her fingernails, full mouth, diamond nose stud and penciled eyebrows hinted further that she was beyond middle school years.

"Are you hungry?" Clarissa tried, turning and looking over her shoulder, back at her cabin. "Come inside."

The girl pushed up, as if preparing to stand. Then, she knelt toward the ground again.

"This is my cabin," Clarissa said, taking hold of the girl's right forearm and helping her to stand. "I'm renting the cabin."

The girl's eyes were dark brown and full like longan. Her wide-eyed gaze darted from side to side, signaling that she expected to be attacked, struck.

"It's just me," Clarissa shared. "I'm the only one at the cabin."

The girl, her footsteps short and slow, followed Clarissa to the cabin's back porch.

"It's okay," Clarissa said, holding the back door open. "Come on," she told the girl. "It's okay. I'm not going to let anyone hurt you."

"How old are you?" she asked after the girl followed her inside the kitchen.

The girl seemed lost in a catatonic stupor. She peered down at her hands, mud and dirt streaking her skin. Her eyes held pools of tears.

"How old are you," Clarissa tried again, reaching in the cupboard for a drinking glass. She went to the refrigerator and poured the girl a glass of water.

"Sixteen," the girl whispered, gifting Clarissa with an answer and the sound of her gentle, trembling voice. She opened her hands and took the glass of water.

Clarissa swallowed hard. She struggled to disguise her surprise at the girl's soiled appearance. "Are you from around here?" she asked, turning and locking the door. Dread of being watched, targeted, overcame Clarissa. Before she knew it, she was closing and locking the screened kitchen windows. She walked through the entire house, closing and locking the windows. Finally, she returned to the kitchen and looked through the back door window.

When she turned away from the door, she jumped.

The girl was standing so close to her that if she turned any further, she would bump the girl.

Clarissa explored the girl's downturned face. She thought that the girl had the saddest eyes that she'd seen. Her mouth was pulled down, her lower eyelids were darkened. She was overcome with tremors, nearly losing control of the glass, now empty of the water that she had drank absent hesitation.

"Where are you from?" Clarissa asked, looking from the girl to the empty glass.

The girl lowered her head until her chin touched her chest. A second later, raising her head, she looked at the glass, yellow daisies decorating its top edge. Then, after taking in a breath, she bowed her head.

"You can put the glass in the sink," Clarissa said.

The girl walked as if she was tired. After she placed the glass in the sink, she turned, her back pressed against the sink edge, and bowed her head.

"Would you like something to eat, a sandwich, fruit?" Clarissa offered.

"Ye-Ye-Yes," the girl nodded in jerky motions. She glanced up at Clarissa, then just as quickly, she looked at the floor.

Clarissa eyeballed the girl before she walked to the refrigerator and opened the door. One by one, she placed a bowl of sliced pineapple, a pack of cherry vanilla yogurt and a plastic bag filled with thinly sliced smoked turkey on the table. Then, she went to the counter on the other side of the kitchen and picked up a half eaten loaf of wheat bread which she also placed on the table.

"Take your choice," Clarissa smiled.

The girl looked at Clarissa, but didn't move.

"Do you like fruit?"

"Ye-Yes."

"Do you like pineapple?" Clarissa tried. She held the bowl of pineapple out to the girl, extending it as if the fruit was a gift. Then, she went to the silverware drawer, retrieved a fork and gave it to the girl.

"Let's sit down," Clarissa said, pulling out a chair.

Seconds passed before the girl sat in the chair across from Clarissa. She ate the pineapple with care, not the least bit of haste.

Clarissa watched the girl eat in silence. Then, she asked the question that she'd been wanting to ask since she first saw the girl. "What's your name?"

"Trisha," the girl whispered, putting another pineapple bite in her mouth.

"Are you from around here?"

Trisha shook her head from side to side.

"Where are you from?" Clarissa asked, watching Trisha take the side of the fork and cut off another bite of pineapple.

"Indianapolis."

"That's a long way from Georgia," Clarissa said. "Do you have family in Georgia?"

"I didn't get to Georgia because I wanted to visit family," she said, warming up to Clarissa. "Can't be on my own yet. I have to finish high school." A second later, she chewed on her bottom lip and added, "--If I can."

"How did you get to Georgia?"

"I'm from Indianapolis," Trisha repeated.

"Do you like it here?" Clarissa asked, trying to get Trisha to reveal more about herself.

Trisha leaned over the bowl of pineapple and ate the remaining fruit fast. Then, she looked at Clarissa and asked, "Is there anymore water?"

"Help yourself," Clarissa said. "Just get the glass out of the sink and pour yourself water out of the jug in the refrigerator."

A sour, pungent odor stung inside Clarissa's nose when Trisha walked behind her, reaching for the refrigerator door. That's when Clarissa saw how dirty Trisha's spring dress was. The dress was a short sleeve, pink floral with a self-tie belt and a wide bottom that swayed when Trisha walked. The bosom area of the dress was form fitting.

Interspersed with the floral pink were deep dirt and mud stains. "Ho-How long were you out by the cabin?"

"Just one other time," Trisha said, lifting the water jug off the refrigerator shelf and filling her glass. "I apologize for hiding out around your house." She returned the jug to the shelf and closed the refrigerator door.

"No apology needed," Clarissa said, looking at Trisha who was again sitting in the chair across from her.

This time Trisha drank the water faster.

"Do you have sisters and brothers?"

"Yes," Trisha told her. "I have three sisters and three brothers. I'm in the middle." She smiled for the first time.

"Do your sisters and brothers live in Georgia?"

"No," Trisha said shaking her head then standing. She went to the sink and placed the glass inside. "Told you I don't have family in Georgia. Where's the dishwashing liquid?"

"I'll wash the dishes," Clarissa told her.

"No," Trisha tried. "I want to wash them. I made them dirty."

Clarissa looked at Trisha for several seconds, at the dirt and mud on her dress and at the streaks of dirt on her face. "The dishwashing liquid is in that drawer on the right, the drawer just below the sink."

While Trisha washed the dishes, Clarissa sat in the kitchen chair trying to get answers. "Do your parents have friends in Georgia?"

"No. I don't think so," Trisha said, placing the dishes in the dish drainer at the side of the sink. "My family still lives in Indianapolis." She paused. "At least, that's where they lived the last time I saw them."

"Did you run away?"

"I can go now," she told Clarissa, the tremors returning. She walked to the back door.

"Do you know anyone around here?" Clarissa asked, extending her hand. An intrusive psychological heaviness began to drape her. It was accompanied by disturbing images of Trisha hiding alone in the woods, yards away from a hungry crouching bobcat or a snarling wolf. Although she had never seen Trisha before, was in no way indebted to her, she felt responsible for Trisha, if for no other reason than that they were both human beings. "Do you?" Clarissa asked again. "Do you know anyone around here?"

"No."

"Then, stay the night," Clarissa advised. "You can stay here and get a good night of rest." She searched Trisha's face, tried to calm the fear that had risen to her eyes. "You'll be safe here for the night," she assured her. "Come on," Clarissa stood and said, "Let's go upstairs and see if we can find some clothes that fit you. And, you can enjoy a nice shower or warm, relaxing bubble bath and settle in for a restful day and a good night of sleep."

Trisha followed Clarissa around the corner and up the living room stairs, being careful to peer out of the living room curtains on her way to the second floor.

Sensing Trisha's concern, Clarissa said, "I pulled the blinds closed enough to prevent anyone from seeing inside." Pausing, she added, "If I close the curtains all the way, it could make the cabin stand out." Midway up the stairs, she said, "Most of the people out here don't even lock their windows during the day. This is a very peaceful, quiet area."

Once on the second floor, Clarissa went to her bedroom straightaway. Pulling open dresser drawers, she dug through her shirts and pants, hunting for clothes that might fit Trisha. Finally, she looked up.

Trisha stood in the hallway, just outside Clarissa's bedroom. As she had when Clarissa and she had first happened upon each other, she stood with her head bowed. For distraction, she looked at the dirt beneath her fingernails.

"You can come in," Clarissa said.

As if frozen, Trisha didn't move, not so much as half a step. Each time that she looked at the bed, she grimaced and turned away, as if shielding herself from a painful memory.

"Come on," Clarissa said. She stood and turned away from her dresser. "It's okay," she smiled. "You can come in. Remember?" she began. "We came up here to find you something to wear after you enjoy a relaxing shower or bath."

Trisha backed away from Clarissa, shaking her head. She kept backpedaling, one uneven step after another.

"I'm not going to hurt you," Clarissa shared, moving from the edge of her bedroom into the hallway.

Trisha bolted down the hallway, toward the stairs.

"Trisha," Clarissa called out. "I'm not going to hurt you." She ran down the stairs after Trisha, the heels of her shoes clomping against each step. Midway through the living room, inches away from an orange Trelis chair, she grabbed Trisha's left forearm.

Chapter Three

Trisha spun partway around. Then, yanking her arms and shoulders, she pulled away from Clarissa. She ran through the living room like she was outside, bumping the end table closest to the dining room, nearly knocking the table over.

At the kitchen's edge, Clarissa reached for Trisha's right shoulder. But, Trisha sped out of reach.

When Trisha reached the back door, she jerked on the dead bolt lock, desperate to open the door and free herself from Clarissa's presence.

"Trisha," Clarissa screamed, wrestling Trisha's hands away from the shiny dead bolt lock. "I'm not going to hurt you."

Trisha swung her legs back, striking Clarissa. Then, she turned and slapped Clarissa's face, neck, shoulders and arms, swinging wildly.

Clarissa bobbed from side to side, trying to avoid Trisha's blows. She failed miserably. Within seconds, her face, neck and arms were stinging. But, she did not turn Trisha loose. Instead, she pulled and jerked on Trisha's shoulder, working to keep her from unlocking the door and running outside. "Trisha, I am not whoever hurt you. I am not that person," Clarissa begged. "I am not those people. I am not going to hurt you," she said, lowering her voice and pulling Trisha's hand away from the lock.

No longer jerking her body or kicking Clarissa, Trisha stilled. Just-like-that, she froze.

"I was just trying to pick clothes out for you to put on after you take a shower or bath," Clarissa made clear. "I don't want to hurt you."

When Trisha turned, her shoulders were shaking. She grimaced, fighting back tears. Her face looked ugly, all scrunched up, like she believed that there was only a small space on her face for her eyes, nose and mouth to fit.

Clarissa watched Trisha's jaw quake, giving way to tears. "You're safe here," Clarissa assured her. A second later, she asked, "Do you have a boyfriend? Does he hit you?"

"No," Trisha answered, slow tears crawling down her face.

"Then, I don't get it," Clarissa admitted, stepping back and releasing Trisha. "Why are you running?"

Trisha looked at the floor.

"Come on," Clarissa smiled, wrapping her arm over Trisha's shoulders. "Let's go back upstairs and get you some clean clothes. What do you say?" she asked, peering into Trisha's eyes.

Trisha nodded. When she did, two tears dropped off her chin to the floor.

Clarissa took two steps, leading the way. Then, she stopped. "You first."

Trisha's steps stuttered, as if in keeping with her troubled thoughts, before she stepped around Clarissa then in front of her.

"The jeans and the blue and gold t-shirt with the fierce tiger on the front," Trisha said, pointing inside Clarissa's second dresser drawer.

"And," Clarissa smiled, pulling the jeans and t-shirt out of the drawer and handing them to Trisha. "Here are underwear and a bra," she added, reaching inside the top drawer.

"The bathroom is across the hall," Clarissa told her. "When you come out of the bathroom, feel free to bring your dress and dirty underwear with you. You can wash and dry the clothes tonight. And," she added. "Help yourself to the underarm deodorant and lotion on the bathroom vanity. I mean that," she said, hoping to wear away any doubt that Trisha might have. "There's shampoo and hair conditioner in the shower that you can use too."

"Thank you," Trisha said, taking the jeans, t-shirt, underwear and bra and walking across the hall to the bathroom.

"There's also a bathroom in here," Clarissa said, exiting her bedroom and walking down the hall to one of the two guest bedrooms. She'd initially thought about taking Trisha into one of the guest bedrooms when they first arrived upstairs. But, Trisha's anxiety told her that asking her to take a shower or bath in a room with a bed wasn't a good idea.

"Can I go in there?" Trisha asked, glancing inside the guest bedroom that was next to Clarissa's bedroom, the guest bedroom furthest away from the living room stairs.

"Sure," Clarissa said, surprised at Trisha's ease with being in the room. After Trisha's earlier outburst, she was certain that a room with a bed would be a trauma trigger.

Stepping around Trisha, Clarissa entered the guest bedroom and walked into the en suite. She called out from inside the spacious bathroom, her voice echoing. "There are plenty of towels in here." She smiled at the green towels and wash rags hanging from the towel rack above the toilet.

"Thank you," Trisha smiled, pulling the jeans, t-shirt, underwear and bra against her chest. "Thank you very much."

"You're welcome," Clarissa said, patting Trisha's back. "It's all yours," she added as she exited the bathroom. "And, again, help yourself."

"Thank you," Trisha nodded before she entered the bathroom, closed and locked the door. She pulled on the knob several times, ensuring that the door really was locked. Turning, she scanned the bathroom for a window. There wasn't one.

That's when Trisha pulled off her clothes, revealing a patchwork of bruises, some as large as a man's palm, all a brownish yellow. She sat on the toilet and peed, her knees touching, her heels going out in opposite directions, while water filled the tub. Her bladder ached while she peed, result of her forcing herself not to urinate while she ran and hid in the woods before she came upon Clarissa's cabin.

Her hand pressed down on the toilet handle real slow. Although Clarissa had been kind to her, Trisha believed that she had to be careful. She didn't want to make noise, let Clarissa know what she was doing.

Lifting the body wash at the side of the tub beneath her nose and flipping the top up, she inhaled. She smiled at the gentle, floral scent. Then, she turned the body wash over and poured a cup of the scented liquid into the tub.

Water splashed against the body wash, filling the bathroom with the sweetest scent. Trisha sunk down in the water and told herself, that as good as it felt inside the cabin, she wasn't safe.

While Trisha took a warm bubble bath, Clarissa hurried downstairs and grabbed her silver laptop. Back upstairs in the second floor office, she pushed her laptop open and typed "Indianapolis runaways" into the search bar. Information on missing children, exploited children, teen safety and runaway and homeless shelters came up right away.

Next, she typed "Trisha, Indianapolis runaway" into the search bar. Several news stories about missing teenage girls from Indianapolis came up. Clarissa sat back in the chair and gawked at the next two headlines, "Cop Charged with Sex Trafficking" and "Police Sergeant Accused of Sex Trafficking".

Clarissa clicked on each of the stories. Her shoulders quaked when she looked at pictures of the cops, their black officer caps placed squarely atop their heads. None of the girls in the Indianapolis runaway news stories looked like the Trisha who was in her guest bathroom.

Half an hour later, dirt no longer part of her appearance, Trisha opened the bathroom door and entered the guest bedroom.

As soon as Clarissa heard Trisha moving in the guest bedroom, she closed the laptop and pushed her chair away from the desk. But, she didn't walk into the guest bedroom, preferring to gift Trisha with privacy.

"Are there police out here?" Trisha asked as soon as she stepped into the hallway.

Clarissa left the second floor office and, walking down the hallway to the guest bedroom, she leaned against the hall credenza. "There's a police station about thirty miles from here. But, like I told you, this is a quiet area." She shrugged. "Nothing happens out here." She looked at Trisha, her gaze going over the t-shirt and jeans, and she smiled. "You look relaxed and refreshed."

"Feel that way too," Trisha said. "Thank you again."

"You're very welcome." A second later, Clarissa asked, "Are you okay with going back downstairs or do you want to stay up here?"

"It's your house. I'll go wherever you tell me."

"You have choices," Clarissa told her. "You always have a choice."

Trisha rolled her eyes and turned away from Clarissa. "We can go downstairs."

They descended the stairs, one behind the other, Clarissa leading the way. They didn't stop until they entered the kitchen.

"I like tea," Clarissa said, reaching into the cupboard above the sink.

"What kinda tea?"

"Well," Clarissa began. "There's lemon herbal, papaya, guava and orange herbal." Glancing over her shoulder, she asked, "Do any of those flavors appeal to you?"

"Orange herbal sounds good."

"Okay," Clarissa said, pulling a box of orange herbal tea and a box of papaya tea out of the cupboard. Next, she grabbed two ceramic drinking cups out of the cupboard.

The longer that Trisha stood behind her, the more questions surfaced in Clarissa's mind. "Forgot to remind you to bring your clothes with you before we came downstairs. The washer and dryer are in the basement." She tilted her head toward the kitchen's back stairwell. "Those stairs behind that open door lead to the basement." She looked at Trisha. "You can go get your summer dress and the underwear that you had on when you first got here and put them in the washer. Just turn the washing machine to 'light delicates' and you'll be set."

Clarissa put a pot of water on the stove while Trisha went upstairs and got her dirty clothes.

"Laundry detergent is in the basement on the shelf above the washing machine," Clarissa called out when Trisha returned to the kitchen, the stinging, pungent odor from Trisha's dirty clothes filling the air.

"Thank you," Trisha said, tucking her dress and underwear in the crease of her arm.

Absent forethought, Clarissa went to the back door and peered through the window. The most that she saw were squirrels and birds playing in the backyard trees. This time, the space next to her car was empty, a sight that brought a smile to Clarissa's face.

Next, Clarissa entered the living room and peered through the blinds. She even walked up on the small landing at the foot of the living room stairs and looked out of that window. The retired couple living in the cabin two hundred yards to the left of her cabin were outside working in their front yard, trimming the hedges and watering the dahlias, zinnias and daisies lining their walkway. At the front of Clarissa's cabin were more birds and squirrels playing. Before she closed the blinds, she saw a couple that she hadn't seen before riding mountain bikes up the dirt road that weaved in front of her cabin.

"I'll be back inside in a second," Clarissa yelled down the basement stairs. "I'm just running out to my car. I'll be right back," she told Trisha.

She grabbed her car keys off the living room end table. Then, she went outside to her car and, putting the car in reverse, she turned the back end of her car away from the dirt road. She didn't know why, but she felt relieved knowing that her car's license plate couldn't be seen from the road.

Trisha was still in the basement when Clarissa returned to the cabin and locked the back door, returning the bolt to its locked position. "Are you okay down there?" she asked, jogging down the basement stairs.

"Yes," Trisha said. She stood in the middle of the basement, arms crossed, staring at the ceiling.

"Well, the tea water is boiling. Come on up and enjoy a cup of tea."

"Okay," Trisha said.

They sat on the living room sofa drinking hot tea. "Did you soak your feet while in the bath?" Clarissa asked.

"The bath felt so good," Trisha told her, closing her eyes and revisiting the cleansing until she felt warmth rush over her shoulders. "I hadn't taken a bath in months," she added, her eyes again open. "It feels so good to be able to do what I want, to feel free."

"Your feet must have been aching with all the walking that you must have had to do just to reach this cabin."

"They were. My feet were stinging like crazy. So many times while I was outside, I thought my feet were going to literally break."

Glancing at Trisha's bare feet, chipped purple polish spotting her uneven toenails, Clarissa put her tea cup on the end table and stood from the sofa. "Let me go get you some ankle socks."

"No," Trisha begged, grabbing Clarissa's forearm.

Force of Trisha's grasp caused Clarissa to stumble backward. When she regained her balance, her attention went toward the sofa.

In response to Clarissa's unwanted attention, Trisha jerked the hand that she had grabbed Clarissa with toward her chest. "I apologize for grabbing you." Her gaze, like the guilt that she felt, went up to where Clarissa stood.

"It's okay," Clarissa said, eyeballing Trisha. She stepped back. "Are your feet cold?"

"Yes."

"Socks it is then," Clarissa said, giving Trisha a suspicious glance before she hurried up the stairs. When she came back downstairs, she held two sporty ankle socks.

"Here you go," she said, tossing the socks into Trisha's lap.

"Thanks." Trisha's mouth went straight, not the intimation of a smile. Her fingers rubbed the black and yellow lines that decorated the socks' top edge.

"Just how far did you walk to get to this cabin?" Clarissa asked, sitting on the sofa next to Trisha.

"Miles." Trisha abandoned her interest in the socks. She sipped the tea and relaxed into the heat that seeped off the cup onto her palms. "Miles."

"Did someone hurt you?" Clarissa tried, looking at the stairwell, refusing to turn toward Trisha, reluctant to jab her with even a hint of embarrassment.

"It's nothing for you to worry about," Trisha said. She turned away from Clarissa and faced the living room window.

"Is someone chasing you?"

"Please," Trisha begged, still facing the window. "Stop asking me these questions."

Clarissa stood. She walked to the high definition television hanging on the wall across the room close to the stairwell. "Do you want to watch a television show?" She turned toward Trisha who continued to look toward the window. "This cabin TV has Fenzi," she smiled. "There are some good movies on Fenzi and Tuvi." She chuckled. "I've been watching those channels over the last few months back at my permanent home."

"You can see what's on," Trisha said, turning away from the window and looking at the television.

"Got any favorite Fenzi shows?"

"What's Fenzi?" Trisha asked. "I don't know what Fenzi is."

Clarissa leaned her head to the side, as if preparing to take a picture. "Are you serious?" she asked, disbelieving that anyone as young as Trisha didn't know what Fenzi was.

"I'm serious," Trisha said. "My family doesn't watch much TV. What is Fenzi?"

"It's like a software program that lets you watch streaming TV shows and movies." Clarissa pulled her Fenzi stick out of the back of the TV. "Here," she said, walking toward Trisha. "This is a Fenzi stick."

"It's small," Trisha said, standing and walking to within inches of Clarissa. "Does it work like another cable channel?"

"Kind of," Clarissa answered. "I guess that it does. I guess that you could say that."

"Do you have Fenzi favorites?"

"Let me plug it back in and we can see what's on Tuvi. That's one of my favorites for movies. Tuvi shows lots of old movies going back to the 1980s and 1990s," Clarissa said, plugging the Fenzi stick into the back of the TV again. "If we don't see anything interesting on Tuvi, we can see if there are any Fenzi TV series that you might like."

"Is *The Quad* on Fenzi? Would be dope to see their latest shows," Trisha said, dropping her guard and growing more relaxed.

"*The Quad* on the BET channel, the show that centers on Georgia A&M?"

"Yes," Trisha laughed.

"*The Quad* has been off TV since 2018. It stopped running two years ago."

Trisha lowered her gaze, then started back stepping.

"No. No. No," Clarissa said, reaching for Trisha's wrist. "It's fine. You didn't know." She peered at Trisha, wondering where she had been over the last two years, curious as to why she seemed to be hiding something.

Clarissa turned and faced the television, picking the remote control up and clicking over to Tuvi. She started flipping through channels.

"I saw that movie when I was a kid," Trisha said, pointing to the television, as she read the overview of a movie starring Denzel Washington.

"*Crimson Tide* is a good movie," Clarissa smiled, also reading the movie's overview. "I actually watched *Crimson Tide* when I first got here. I was trying to write when I came across *Crimson Tide* on Tuvi and decided to watch it." She smiled. "It had been years since I'd seen the movie. Denzel Washington, Gene Hackman and the other actors did an amazing job bringing the story to life."

"They did," Trisha nodded. Seconds later, she asked, "Is the TV series *The Middle* on Fenzi? I love that show," she smiled. "My sisters and I used to watch that show. I bet those new episodes are funny."

"*The Middle*," Clarissa said. "How about that?" she grinned. "I used to watch that show too. It was about a family living in Indiana. I love the actress, Patricia Heaton, who played the mother on that show. But," Clarissa said, "*The Middle* doesn't come on TV anymore. It stopped airing new episodes two years ago."

Even before she turned, Clarissa knew that Trisha was looking at the floor. She felt a tinge of guilt. "I apologize. Here," she said, holding the remote out to Trisha. "How about you turn the channels and find something that you want to watch." She laughed. "After all, looks like we enjoy the same types of TV shows and movies."

"No. You pick the show."

"No, here," Clarissa said, pushing the remote toward Trisha. "I don't have to make all of the decisions. You can call some of the shots."

Trisha fumbled with the remote. Then, she started flipping through channels. "This remote is sweet," she chuckled. "Is *Black Panther* on here?"

"It might be on one of the pay channels," Clarissa said. "I loved that movie too."

"How about we watch the movie, *Joy*?" Trisha asked, looking at Jennifer Lawrence's face on the film poster as the actress peered up at, what appeared to be, falling snow. "I saw that movie a few years ago, really liked it. Have you seen it?"

"If I did, I don't recall," Clarissa lied, wanting to settle on a show rather than spend more time watching Trisha flip through channels.

"It's about a woman who starts her own business," Trisha said, shaking her head. "I love a strong, independent woman."

"So, do I," Clarissa said. "Let's watch *Joy*."

Trisha stared at the remote.

"Click the OK button," Clarissa told her.

While they waited for the movie to start, Clarissa tried a new approach. "Want to grab something to snack on from the kitchen? Think that I have popcorn, if you have a taste for popcorn."

"I'm fine," Trisha said. "I've eaten more today than I've eaten in a long time."

"Well, let me know if you get hungry. Feel free to grab food from the refrigerator or the cabinets."

"Thank you. You're very kind. Thanks for being so nice to me."

"Absolutely," Clarissa said. "It's the only way to be."

"That would be nice." Trisha gazed across the room at the empty space above the television.

"What would be nice?"

"It would be nice if everyone was like you, if everyone thought the way that you do. You know?" Trisha shrugged. "About being nice to everyone."

"Who in the world wouldn't be nice to you?"

"Some people," Trisha said, walking to the sofa and sitting near the window. She held the socks for awhile before she pulled them over her feet.

"Who wouldn't be kind to you?" Clarissa asked, sitting on the opposite end of the sofa.

"Some people," Trisha said, lifting her tea cup off the end table and holding it in her hand.

"No one has ever hit you, have they?" Clarissa asked, picking her tea cup up and taking a sip of the tea.

"My life isn't easy anymore," Trisha admitted. Standing, she walked to the television and picked up the remote which she brought back to the sofa. As soon as she sat on the sofa again, she turned the television volume up. "That's Joy," she said, pointing to the petite blonde on the television screen.

"Okay," Clarissa said. "Think I'm gonna love this story. It sounds inspiring."

"Joy wins in the end."

"You like movies with happy endings?"

"I want to see a whole lot of women win. I want to see women finally start to win a lot," Trisha said.

"Is your mother an independent woman? Does she go after what she wants?"

A scowl formed at the center of Trisha's forehead. "Can we leave my mother out of our conversations?"

"Just one more question."

Trisha found nothing more to give Clarissa except silence.

"Does your mother know where you are?"

"I thought you already asked me that?" Trisha stammered, twisting her mouth and rolling her eyes.

"If I did, I forgot. I'd really like to know."

"You keep asking me so many questions," Trisha frowned. "I thought we were going to watch the movie. Isn't that what you said you wanted to do?" She didn't wait for Clarissa to answer. Instead, she rolled her eyes and continued, "I know that's what you said. Yes," she nodded sharply. "That's what you said. You said you wanted to watch the movie. But, here you are asking me a load of questions. Here you are pounding me with question after question."

Clarissa fell back against the sofa. Loose strands of hair near her forehead blew up when she released a thick breath. She crossed her legs and arms and pleaded, "Just this one last question."

Trisha pushed her lips together with such force that her mouth hurt. "No," she yelled. "My mother doesn't know where I am, and I know that I already told you that." She stared at the side of Clarissa's head. "When we were in the kitchen, I told you that my mother doesn't know where I am."

"We never talked about your mother before."

"I could swear we did. You started pestering me with questions as soon as I came in this cabin. You just want to keep asking me questions. And, you can't even change anything. You can't make anything better."

"Are you in trouble?"

"Thought the question about my mother was the last stupid question that you were going to ask?"

"I want you to be safe," Clarissa said, unfolding her arms. "And, believe it or not, the more that you tell me, the more I can do to ensure that you're safe while you're here." She paused. "While I was out for my morning run today, I saw a dirty van on the main road." She gave Trisha a probing glance.

Trisha turned away from Clarissa, no longer frowning. Then, she quickly faced Clarissa again. This time, her brows were raised. "What time did you see the van?"

Chapter Four

"It was around eight o'clock this morning."

"Who was driving the van?"

"Couldn't see the driver from where I was running on the dirt road." Clarissa stood and walked toward the living room window. "Come here. I'll show you," she said, opening the blinds.

Trisha almost leaped off the sofa. She stood just behind Clarissa's right shoulder.

"Come around, so that you can see," Clarissa told her, feeling the heat from Trisha's body on her shoulder.

Trisha didn't move.

"There's no one or anything outside the window except for the birds and the squirrels."

Trisha stepped to Clarissa's side and, while standing right next to Clarissa, she looked out the window at the dirt road.

"How far down does that road go?"

"Miles," Clarissa told her. "It goes all the way to the highway. You can even get to the river from that road. You'll have to veer off to the right, crossing over the two lane highway. But, you can get to the Chattahoochee River from that little dirt road."

Trisha went up on her toes. "It doesn't look wide enough for a big van to get down."

"It's not," Clarissa said. "That's another thing that I like about this cabin. I come here if it's been a long while since I've come up with an idea for a new novel." She paused. "No," she added, peering out at the road. "I come here when I've been struggling to start putting a story on paper, to actually start writing, even if I already have a story idea." Turning and facing Trisha, she said, "I'm a novelist, have been since I was twelve years old. But," she revealed, "Sometimes I struggle."

"I struggle sometimes too," Trisha shared. "Just not because I can't find something to write about."

"But, no," Clarissa said, turning away from Trisha, "A big truck or a large van can't fit down the dirt road, at least not without driving up on the grass."

"How far is the two lane highway from here?" Trisha asked.

"About a mile away."

"Am I really safe here?"

"I used to be in the Navy," Clarissa told her. "I have special training." She looked out the window. "I also learned more fighting and defensive skills on my own after I was honorably discharged from the Navy."

"I know how to fight too," Trisha said. "I learned how to fight on the streets. But, it's hard to defend yourself against four men."

"Which four men?"

"Never mind," Trisha responded, turning away from the window.

"No," Clarissa said. "Tell me." She reached for Trisha's hand. "We need to talk about this. You can't bury whatever happened to you forever."

"I don't know you," Trisha said, pulling her hand out of Clarissa's grasp.

"I know that I'm a woman who has been hurt by men before," Clarissa shared.

"You live in this nice cabin. You have a good car. You even have a second home," Trisha frowned. "You aren't running from anyone," she snapped. "You don't have anyone after you."

"Who's after you?"

"Can we just watch the movie?" Trisha yelled. "I appreciate everything you've done for me. But, please, stop asking me so many questions. I don't even know you. Stop being nosy. All I need is enough time to figure out what to do next, and then I'll be gone. I just need to rest for awhile. Please." Turning, she muttered, "Damn."

"If you don't tell me who's after you, how will I know who to protect you from?" Clarissa stared at Trisha, daring her to meet her glance. "I could actually invite the person who's after you inside the cabin and not even know it."

"Some guys," Trisha shrugged.

"Are these guys in a dirty, white van?"

"I think that was them," Trisha nodded.

"The van had Texas license plates," Clarissa added, noticing that the pace of her heartbeat had picked up. She worked not to let her mind fill with dread. "It looked strange, like whoever was inside the van wasn't from around here. The van was too dirty to be a rental."

"How long can I stay here?" Trisha asked, fidgeting with her fingers.

"As long as you need to. But, I'm only renting this cabin for another week."

"I can't stay here without you," Trisha exclaimed. "I don't have any money."

"Don't worry," Clarissa told her. "I won't leave you stranded." She looked right at Trisha. "But, you have to tell me everything. You have to tell me who you're running from, what this person did to you. I have to know why you're running."

"Do you know the men who were driving the van? Did you talk to them? Have you met them before?" Clinching her jaw, Clarissa added, "If you don't tell me everything you know, I'll have to turn you over to the police." Tossing her hands up, she said, "I won't be able to help you if you don't tell me everything."

"No. No," Trisha begged. "Don't turn me over to the police. I could be put in a home until my parents come get me. I'd become part of the system. Plus, there are too many cops who are dirty." She shook her head, "There are good cops. But, there are crooked cops too. Taking me to the police could put me in worse danger. And this is a small town," she said. "Who knows how dirty these cops out here are."

With a pinch of her lip, Clarissa delayed an outburst. Yet, she was unable to stop her jaw muscles from tightening and her neck from feeling warm. This wasn't what she had wanted. She'd hoped for a productive day of writing, not to be forced to deal with a strange teenager's mounting troubles. After a pause, she gave a slow answer. While she spoke, she kept the volume in her voice even. "Don't ask me why, but I trust you. And, it's clear that you need help." After a sigh, she told Trisha, "To answer your earlier question, I didn't see who was driving the van."

Trisha released a deep breath. She leaned toward Clarissa. "Everything is on the line for me." For the first time, she looked right at Clarissa, not flinching, not turning away. Shaking her head, she said, "There's too much on the line for me. I really need to know who was in that van." Wringing her hands, she added, "I have to know who was in that van."

Clarissa stepped back. "You have a lot on the line?" she snapped. "So do I. If you're not safe, do you think that I'm safe while you're here?" She stared at Trisha. "Do you?"

"There has never been anyone who I could trust, not one hundred percent." Pacing the floor in a small circle, she added, "Not even my mother."

Clarissa peered at her.

"Yes, my mother," Trisha said, standing still. "The only thing that my mother gave me was a blind eye after she saw her pitiful oldest brother, my uncle, with his hands up the center of my thighs." She bowed her head.

"We were sitting in the kitchen. I was six years old." Shaking her head, she added, "Only six years old. With one hand, my uncle sat me on his lap on a kitchen chair, holding me as I squirmed. With his other hand, he molested me. He did it as if he was playing a freaking game." She frowned. "It meant nothing to him. Nothing," she yelled. "And," she added, "It obviously didn't mean anything to my mother. She just looked at us, then turned and left the kitchen."

"That's awful. That's horrible," Clarissa said, peering into the face of her own troubled past. Hearing Trisha's trauma worked like a strong impulse, pushing Clarissa to share her own similar trauma. "I was molested as a child too. A neighbor," she told Trisha. "He was a high school football star, celebrated by an entire school, name in the local newspaper and all. And," she added, "He molested young girls." Seconds later, she said, "I was nine years old. My siblings and I had just moved from Ohio to Tennessee."

"Did your mother help you?"

"My mother passed when I was seven years old."

"Were you close to your mother?" Trisha asked.

"My mother was sick a lot, so I didn't get to know the *real* her much." She paused. "I wish that I had gotten to know my mother more."

"My mother isn't dead, but we barely know each other. I stopped trusting my mother after she saw her poor excuse for a brother molesting me and just walked off as if she hadn't seen anything, leaving me in danger." Seconds later, she said, "He could have done anything to me. My mother didn't care."

"Do you think that the experience set you up for whatever you're dealing with now?"

"No. No. No," Trisha said.

"Did your uncle only touch you once?" As much as she hated asking the question, Clarissa wanted to know how pervasive the abuse that Trisha suffered was. She was overcome with an eerie curiosity. It was as if she thought knowing what happened to Trisha would save her from the pain birthed from her own childhood sexual traumas.

"It went on for about two years." She gritted her teeth. "I hate that I didn't stop him." She grimaced. "The worst part was acting like nothing had happened when we were at family events. After a year of the abuse, I started telling my parents that I was sick the day before we were supposed to visit my grandparents'. I did it on Thanksgiving, Christmas, Easter, a family barbecue, you name it." She looked at Clarissa. "I didn't want to see my uncle and act like everything was cool anymore."

"When's the last time you saw your uncle?"

"About eight years ago,"

"Good," Clarissa said. "You don't need to keep being traumatized. No one needs that," she said. "For me, it was hard enough to grow up in the same neighborhood that the guy who molested me lived in. But, I am glad that I told my siblings and my father right away. My dad spoke with the guy and let him know that if he ever bothered me again, he'd make him regret it for the rest of his life. I also was never allowed to spend a night over anyone else's house, except for family my dad knew well, after that."

"You seem okay."

"I've done a lot of inner work over the years, and not just to heal from the sexual abuse. I did a lot of inner work to heal from false perceptions." She chuckled. "I still do inner work. I'm not real religious, but I sure do love the Lord. I want to step back into my true self, the Self the Creator brought into existence."

"Whatever that is," Trisha said.

"Whatever what is?"

"Your true self."

"We're all trying to realize we never left our one, true home," Clarissa told her.

"I just want to get home so I can get a job and save up enough money to get an apartment."

"Are you close to your father?"

"Yes. He's dope," Trisha said. "He's open minded. My mom's super religious. She thinks life should only go a certain way. It's like she's lost in the 1950s or something. Probably why she didn't protect me from her brother. I wouldn't be shocked if she told herself what she saw wasn't happening just so she could live in a make-believe world of purity."

"Do your parents know who you're running from?"

"No," Trisha said, her jaw clenching. She looked up at the ceiling. Finally, she turned her head sideways, peered across the room and revealed, "I was kidnapped." Her voice came out flat, as if she was talking about someone else. Then, her body betrayed her as her hands started to tremble. She hid them behind her back.

"Were you at home when you were kidnapped--"

"--I was at work. Well," she continued. "I was just leaving work." She paused. "This guy asked me if I wanted to earn some extra cash." She lowered then shook her head. "Of course, I said - yes. That's when the guy smiled and handed me a brochure with a website URL on it. There were models on the front and back of the brochure. Inside the brochure, were testimonials from models saying how happy they were earning thousands of dollars from modeling. A few of the testimonials even said that the women, all young, had made thousands of dollars from acting jobs that they got after they started working with the modeling company. I was excited," she told Clarissa. "As soon as I got home, I pulled up the website on my laptop."

"I was so naive, so stupid," she stammered. "Damn, was I dumb. I never figured myself for being naive. I've never been that stupid. It's not like I grew up in a perfect family. It's not like I'd never seen a hard time. Shit. I'd seen my share of con artists. I could spot a scam a mile away. But, not this time. It was all that modeling talk." She felt tired, like she'd been standing near the cabin window for an hour. Before she knew it, she had returned to the sofa. She sat close to the window.

"How old were you?"

"Fourteen."

"And you were working?"

"Yes. I was working a part-time job at the mall. My mama told me that she wasn't feeding freeloaders. So, I got a job."

"And, your dad?"

"He worked a lot. He went on a lot of business trips. My dad's a corporate executive. He's a senior compliance officer at a major firm."

"Oh," Clarissa said. "So, your mom had the primary job of caring for you and your siblings." She paused. "That couldn't have been easy for your mom," she said, following Trisha to the sofa and sitting.

"Yeah, I guess," Trisha said, turning away from Clarissa.

"So, you looked up the modeling agency on your laptop as soon as you got home that day?"

"Yes. It looked legit. Two days passed before I saw the guy again. He showed up outside the mall, right outside the store that I worked as a cashier at. It was like he knew the days and hours when I worked."

Clarissa felt the hair rise on her arms. Her skin felt tight. It unnerved her when she turned and saw Trisha hugging herself. She watched Trisha start to rock back and forth. It looked like an unconscious movement, as if

Trisha didn't even know that she was moving forward and then slowly backward, going nowhere, being stuck.

Chapter Five

"Do you want to take a break from telling me what happened? Maybe a five minute break?" Clarissa asked. She had tired of watching Trisha rock. She was willing to do or say anything to get Trisha to sit still, to just be still.

"No. I'm going to finish telling you everything. If I stop, I might never talk about it again."

"Okay," Clarissa said, picking the remote up and turning the television off. "I'm listening. "

"The guy asked me how I was doing and how work was. Then, he asked me if I loved my job." She shrugged. "I told him that my job was okay. It gave me money to spend. Then, he asked me if I'd like to make more money, and if I'd read the brochure." She squinted. "I should have known to leave right then. But, I was so stupid."

"You were young."

"I was stupid," Trisha exclaimed. She pounded her fist into her palm. "The guy told me that the head of the modeling agency was interviewing for new models at a small office building less than a mile from the mall. It was in a nice area. He said that the interviews were being held that Saturday." She shrugged. "I figured, what could

I lose? So, I went." She sighed. "I lied and told my mother that I was going over a friend's. Damn. Talk about a regret," she added, twisting her mouth.

"Was anyone at that small office building when you got there that Saturday?"

"Yes. Oh, yes," Trisha nodded. "There were eight to ten other girls there. They were beautiful, thin girls. They looked like real models. I thought that they'd get hired and that I wouldn't." She sighed, her shoulders caving, as if the strength had gone out of them. "I wish I had never gone to that place." Tears pooled beneath her eyes then flowed, leaving a wet line on each side of her face. Tears didn't stop rolling until they landed in her lap, against the tops of her balled hands.

"I never saw my family again," she cried.

Clarissa wrapped her arms around Trisha's shoulders, pulling her close. "We're going to get you back home."

A moment later, Clarissa sat up and patted Trisha's hand. She softened her voice and asked, "Where did the guy take you?"

"There were three guys in a room behind the office that me and some other girls were sitting in," Trisha said. "They came out as soon as the other guy finished all of the bogus interviews. After the sham interviews, we were photographed. Then, the guys said that we were all hired and asked us if we wanted to go to lunch." She groaned. "I said - yes. All of us girls said - yes. And, that was the start of it all."

"Did you all go to lunch?"

"Not to a restaurant. The guys told us that time was limited and that it would be best to get something to eat on the go. We were supposed to be going to a modeling shoot that day at a better location across town. They put us up in a posh hotel near the airport. I swear, I don't remember much else from that day. All I know," Trisha said, "Is that I went out. It was like I just passed out about half an hour after we got to the hotel. Later I learned that I had been drugged. I actually think that they put something in our food. They took us back to the hotel to eat because they didn't want to risk us having a bad reaction to the drugs. They didn't want us to fall out in the restaurant and attract attention."

"You could be right," Clarissa said.

"Late that night, I woke up feeling real heavy, real foggy. My arms felt like they weighed fifty pounds each. I couldn't even lift my arms. I still don't know what they gave me. Anyhow, a middle aged piece-of-shit guy was laying naked on the bed next to me. I was naked too." Her body shook, as if reacting to the memory of the trauma. "That's when I knew for sure that something was wrong, way way wrong. But, it was too late," she wept.

Clarissa leaned over and hugged her. "You did the best that you could."

Trisha sat up, pulling away from Clarissa. "No, I didn't," she shouted. "I didn't do the best that I could. I was stupid, so stupid."

Clarissa rubbed Trisha's shoulder, refusing to abandon comforting her.

"It went on like that for all of the next week," she cried. "I was so close to home, but I couldn't get home. I couldn't get free," she cried. "Then, they took us out of state. They made us prostitute ourselves in different places. I got raped over and over. These older men, probably husbands and fathers, someone's brothers and sons, had sex with me and the other girls like it was their right, their absolute right, to have sex with whoever they wanted to have sex with." It surprised her when she looked into her lap and saw that her hands had clenched into fists. "I will never understand how grown men, old enough to be both of our fathers, could even want to have sex with girls who are barely teenagers, some who haven't even reached puberty." She shook her clenched fists.

"Sick," Clarissa said. "And, these people don't seek help. They have degrees, a great financial setup and are connected." She twisted her mouth. "They don't care about other people enough." She shook her head. "They just don't and nothing is rarely done to them because of their connections, because of who they know and because of who their clients are." She paused, as if digesting what she'd just said. "How long were you held captive?"

"Two years. I tried to run away. The second time I tried to run away, I was beaten for a solid twenty minutes." She wept, her shoulders trembling. "Have you ever been beaten, I mean beaten with a man's fists, for twenty straight minutes?" After a long pause, she continued, "I didn't try to run away again until four days ago. I've been running for four straight days. I've never been so terrified. I kept thinking that the men would catch me. It was so scary. I really thought they would catch me, and if not them, some other sick man."

"Do you know where the other girls are?"

"Four of us escaped. The last place where we were held is about sixty miles from here, closer to Atlanta. We thought it was best if we split up and ran in different directions. We're all tough," she said. "I really think all four of us will make it."

"You were in a sex slave trafficking outfit," Clarissa told her. "I'm so glad that you got out. We're going to get you home safely."

"I ran and walked the whole way on foot. No way was I getting in anybody's car. Those guys know a lot of people. They have clients all over the world. I wasn't about to risk being found."

"Do you think that the guys in the van saw you while you were out on the road earlier today or maybe yesterday?"

Trisha wrapped her arms around herself and started rocking back and forth. Except for her deliberate rocking, she looked cold, frozen with fear.

"It's okay." Hugging her, Clarissa's said, "I'll get you to the authorities."

"What authorities?" Trisha asked, her voice quaking.

"The police."

"No. No. No," Trisha responded, shaking her head. "Like I told you before, I'm not going to any police. There are people in the police who are involved in sex trafficking. Most cops aren't, but I've got too much at stake. I'm not willing to roll the dice. There are people in governments, wealthy people, business people, people in high places with lots of money who are involved in it. They're clients. They're customers. No," she said, shaking her head again. "I'm not going to the police. I want to go home."

"But, these men, and, who knows, there might be women involved in it too, who these hustlers know could come looking for you once you get home. They already work that area," Clarissa reminded her. "That's where they found you and the other girls at the interview place. Remember?"

"Yes," Trisha moaned. "Well," she began, looking up at Clarissa, searching her face for answers. "Where can I go? Where will I be safe?"

"There are shelters and homes for girls and women who have fled sex slave trafficking," Clarissa told her. "I'll check around. I won't use any resources that will connect us to the cabin," she assured Trisha. "Thanks to my Navy days, I know how to do things and not create footprints."

Trisha's shoulders relaxed, lowered into a gentler spot. She even started to feel a knot work its way out of the back of her neck.

"But, we should pack, just in case we have to leave in a hurry. After all," Clarissa said, "We don't know where those men who I saw in the van this morning are. Hopefully, they're in Atlanta."

"Okay," Trisha agreed. "But, I'm not going to the shelter without Amber, Jackie and Wanda."

"Are they the girls you escaped with?"

"Yes," Trisha nodded. "I'm not going to any shelter without them." She looked straight ahead. "I'm not even going home without them."

"Are they from Indianapolis?"

"No. Amber and Jackie are from Atlanta and Wanda is from Philadelphia."

"Okay," Clarissa said, standing. "Let's go pack. Then, let's finish the movie. Watching the movie will help us to relax. It's better to be relaxed than all knotted up, in case we have to make a move for it. And, I want to tell my neighbors to let me know if they see a van and not to tell anyone where I live. The guy who lives in the cabin about two hundred yards from here is a former Navy Seal. He's smart and he's a good guy. His wife is sharp too. They're so sharp that, even as good as we've gotten along the several weeks that I've stayed at the cabin, I know they've checked me out. Probably ran a background check on me." She chuckled. "Thanks to their investigations, they know I'm good. That's the main reason they'll look out for me."

"Okay," Trisha nodded.

"Stay here," Clarissa told her. "Stay here," she repeated, just before she grabbed her keys and hurried outside the cabin. She ran all the way to her neighbor's.

Less than ten minutes later, when Clarissa returned to her cabin, she told Trisha, "I'm going to go upstairs and grab a reinforced lock for my car. I'm also going to turn a camera on, so that I can see what's going on outside the cabin." She paused. "If I had it, I'd put a PTZ camera at two ends of the dirt road, so I'd be able to see someone coming, giving us at least five minutes to get out of here. But," she added, exploring the fear in Trisha's eyes, "We'll be fine. The couple up the road is going to look out for the cabin," she said, working at a smile. Taping Trisha's shoulder, she advised, "Just don't get too comfortable. We'll be out of here first thing in the morning."

Chapter Six

The sky was orange-red when Clarissa scampered down the cabin's living room stairs, her heels barely touching each step, she moved so fast. She hurried through the living room, dining room and kitchen, then unlocked the back door and ran down the four wooden outdoor steps to the trunk of her car. Pressing the key remote, she popped the trunk open. The morning air was crisp, inviting. Quiet solitude made it easy for her to hear herself breathe. Her breath sounded like a clear vent opening and closing, air in - air out.

Despite her efforts, she couldn't stop thinking about the text message that the couple in the cabin next to hers had sent her last night. "Some guys stopped by a few hours after you left yesterday evening," the couple had texted. "They asked who lived in the cabin you're renting. Also asked if we'd seen any teenage girls roaming the area. We told them nothing."

"We're the guys in a van?"

"No. They were in a Mustang. Are you okay?"

"I'm fine. Thanks for the heads up," Clarissa had texted in return.

"Good. Stay safe," the couple texted. "Reach out if you need anything. Every now and then drifters come through here. Probably looking for a quick way to make easy money, maybe rip an unsuspecting renter off. That's probably what the guys in the van you told us you saw were up to."

Now, rushing to the back seat of her car, Clarissa hoped that her reluctance to tell her neighbors about Trisha wouldn't come back to haunt her. The couple had been kind to her since their first meeting. Yet, she only rented the cabin a few weeks out of the year. The limited time that she spent at the cabin didn't offer her complete confidence that she truly knew the couple. For that reason, she wasn't willing to risk sharing Trisha's identity, potentially putting Trisha in danger, not even to the couple living next door.

The text message at the top of her memory, she grabbed a thick, yellow plastic bucket, anti-freeze and two windshield wiper fluid bottles off the floor and tossed them into the trunk. Before she closed the trunk, she grabbed a heavy, green wool blanket.

She placed the blanket across the back seat. Then, she closed and locked the Camry's back door. Hurrying up the wooden steps and back inside the cabin, she raced through the dining room and living room. As soon as she got upstairs, she grabbed her suitcase which she lugged downstairs and outside. She pushed the suitcase inside the trunk.

She was still arranging her suitcase in the trunk when she heard a fallen tree limb break followed by the rustle of leaves less than fifty yards from where she stood. The noise sounded as if it had come from the front of the cabin, over by the dirt road.

"Shit," Clarissa snapped, realizing that she had left her book bag on the living room sofa.

Crouching next to the Camry, she closed and locked the trunk. Then, she snuck back inside the cabin.

Creeping through the cabin in a stooped position, she snatched her book bag off the sofa. Before she reached the cabin's back door again, she was holding her Glock, the safety on.

She threw the book bag on the Camry's front passenger seat. Then, crouching so close to the cabin that her shoulder brushed the brick, she lifted the Glock to her chest and inched to the front of the cabin, her gaze darting. Every few seconds, she turned and looked over her shoulder toward the Camry.

A rabbit stood at the edge of the back yard chewing grass. When the rabbit didn't flinch, Clarissa released a breath. If anyone was out back, she knew that the rabbit would have bolted.

When she turned and faced the front of the cabin again, she swallowed hard. Flattened patches of grass revealed company. She inhaled deeply. She froze until she was certain that she hadn't picked up the scent of a man's cheap cologne.

Inching closer to the front of the cabin, she couldn't stop thinking about the flattened grass patches at the side of the cabin. She saw three more flattened patches the closer that she got to the front porch.

Her hands trembled when she looked closer at the patches. It took her a second to make the shapes out, but she saw what they were; they were footprints.

With a sweeping gaze, she followed the footprints to the dirt road. That's when she removed the Glock's safety. She crouched low and turned the cabin's front corner sharply.

She closed her eyes, overcome with relief, when she saw that the front porch was empty. Then, hearing a branch break on the other side of the dirt road, she crouched again and looked toward the road, squinting to see through the bushes and trees separating the road from the two lane highway below.

Next, she glanced toward her neighbor's house. She frowned when she saw that their cabin lights were out.

Spit went down her throat like a sour gel, she swallowed so hard. Then, she crossed the road to get a better inspection of the trees and bushes. Seconds passed before she convinced herself that she'd seen no one. That's when she returned to the cabin, entering again through the back door.

The first place that she went was upstairs into the guest bedroom. "Wake up. Wake up," she demanded of Trisha, shaking her shoulders.

Trisha pulled her legs up toward her stomach. Then, she lifted the comforter over her shoulder and, yawning, relaxed deeper into sleep.

"Get up," Clarissa shouted. "Get up," she ordered, kicking the side of the bed.

She sunk her fingers into Trisha's shoulder and lifted up. "Get up. Get up," she yelled.

Trisha's body bounced on the bed.

"Get up," Clarissa screamed.

Instead of waking, Trisha kicked her legs frantically.

"Get up," Clarissa tried again, this time with less volume in her voice.

Trisha rocked from side to side. Seconds later, she sat up. Her hair was pulled back in a single braid. "What?" she asked, peering at Clarissa.

"We have to go. We have to leave now."

"What's going on? What's happening?" Trisha asked, pulling her legs over the side of the bed.

"Come on," Clarissa said. "We may not be safe." Grabbing the sides of Trisha's shoulders, she helped Trisha get out of the bed.

A moment later and no longer groggy, Trisha almost ran inside the bathroom.

"Here," Clarissa said, opening the bathroom door. "Put these jeans, this t-shirt and underwear on. There's a pair of clean socks on the bed. Hurry," she told Trisha. "We have to move. We have to get out of here."

"Are we coming back?" Trisha asked less than five minutes later. She was fully dressed, her teeth brushed and her hair re-braided.

"You're fast."

"The last two years taught me to be ready to move at a second's notice," Trisha said. She sat on the bed and pulled on the socks. "Not to mention how I've had to be ready to bolt over the last four days that I've been on the run on foot."

Moments later, the cabin was empty.

"Lay down across the back seat," Clarissa told Trisha. "I hate to make you do that. But, I don't know who's out here, and I don't know who's seen my car."

"What do you want me to do with this grocery bag we brought to the car with us?" Trisha asked, laying down across the seat.

"Please put it on the floor. There's bottled water, fruit, vegetables and peanut butter crackers in the bag, enough food for us to eat until we get to my permanent residence."

"I'm not going anywhere without Amber, Jackie and Wanda," Trisha said. "I'll get out and take my chances on foot before I leave them."

"Okay," Clarissa groaned, pulling out of the driveway and turning left, toward the cabin next door.

"Where are you going?" Trisha asked, raising her head and peering out of the car's back window. She squinted in effort to adjust her vision to the early morning darkness.

"To the neighbor's," she answered, glancing across the road. "Someone was outside the cabin. Could just have been a tourist or someone noising around while they were out for a jog or a walk. We did head in early yesterday. But, those footprints were fresh, like they were created this morning." She shook her head. "Can't risk getting caught."

"Should I stay in the car?" Trisha asked as soon as Clarissa pulled her Camry into the neighbor's gravel side driveway.

"Yes," Clarissa said. "I'm only going up on the porch. I'm not going inside their cabin. And, I'm going to keep watch over the car and the outdoor area."

"Okay," Trisha nodded, laying flat against the back seat again.

"There's another green blanket at the other end of the seat," Clarissa told Trisha. "Cover yourself with that blanket. It's clean and didn't come out of the trunk. I got that blanket out of my cabin's primary bathroom linen closet."

"Okay," Trisha said, reaching for the blanket.

Moments later, Clarissa stood next to her neighbors' cabin. "Don't know what's going on," she revealed. She shook her head. "Never had any trouble like this, and it's usually so quiet out here."

"Crazy world," the man said. "You never know what's going to happen. We'll keep an eye out for anything out of the ordinary."

"Thanks," Clarissa nodded. "I should be in touch later today."

"Okay," the man said. Twisting his mouth, he added, "You were smart to stop by. Like we texted you last night, two guys stopped by yesterday evening asking who lived at the cabin that you stay at and asking if we'd seen any teenage girls."

"We told them that we hadn't seen anything," the man's wife said. "We called you first. But," she shook her head and laughed. "We know that you normally keep your cell phone on mute. So, we texted you."

"Which brings up a point," the man said. "With everything that's going on, it's a good idea for you to keep your phone on sound. We don't expect anything to happen. But, just in case, it's a good idea if you make it easy for us to reach you."

"Agreed," Clarissa nodded.

"Keep your eyes and ears open," the man advised. "You're rarely out here, but we can tell you're honest. We'll look out for you," he added, looking at his wife then again at Clarissa.

With that, Clarissa climbed back inside the Camry and drove toward the road. She turned right and headed toward Atlanta.

"Where to now?" Trisha asked from where she continued to lay down on the back seat.

"You can sit up now," Clarissa said. "Please just keep your head below the window. And where are we headed? We're headed to a gun shop. I want to get another gun that you can use, should we need it. Then," she added. "We're going to spend the day looking for your three friends. After that, we have to get to my place." Glancing in the rearview mirror, she told Trisha, "I know you don't want to risk tipping off crooked cops, but we have to pull in help. I'll contact several sharp people I know I can trust. If you were still on foot, I'd rather you run to a cop and ask someone nearby to go to the police station with you; that way you'd have a witness should anything wrong happen. That's better than being on the street alone," she added. "We can contact the authorities and put out a bulletin in search of your friends from my place." She glanced in the rearview mirror again. "The longer that we stay out here driving around, the more at risk the girls who escaped with you could be and the more at risk we become of getting caught. And," she shared, "As good as I am with a weapon, I don't think that I could take out four grown men who have very bad intentions all by myself."

Chapter Seven

Half an hour later, Clarissa pulled onto a large gravel parking lot. A sign swung back and forth from two metal chains at the top of a grey wood building. The sign read "Mortars Gun Shop". Besides Clarissa's Camry, there were two large trucks, a yellow Volkswagen and a burgundy Ford Ranger in the parking lot.

Trisha stayed in the Camry, hiding beneath the green blanket, while Clarissa entered the gun shop. Figuring that Trisha had never held a gun before, it didn't take Clarissa long to settle on a Ruger nine millimeter handgun.

Trisha was still laying beneath the blanket when Clarissa returned to the car. She put the Ruger in the glove compartment then drove to the back of the gun shop.

"Get out," she told Trisha after she parked the Camry and stepped out of the car, her shoes creating a crunch sound as she walked over the gravel at the far rear of the shop.

"What are we doing?" Trisha asked.

"I want you to get used to holding this gun. And, you're going to start aiming the gun and learning to move with the weapon in your hand."

"Is the gun heavy?" Trisha asked, sitting up and opening the Camry's back passenger door.

"Come see for yourself." Clarissa smiled, recalling the first time that she held a gun. That was more than six years ago. She'd been pressing her way through Navy boot camp.

Her steps slow and steady, Trisha took her time approaching Clarissa. She kept her gaze fixed on the gun that Clarissa held in her hand, the gun's front sight aimed toward the ground.

"Stand here," Clarissa directed, pointing toward the space to her left.

While Trisha walked to her side, Clarissa turned and looked over her shoulder. She exhaled when she saw the gun shop parking lot empty. Only two other factors gave her relief, the fact that both Trisha and she now had a gun and the fact that they stood more than two hundred yards away from the wood gun shop.

Turning back around, she placed the gun in Trisha's hand. Then, she raised Trisha's arms. As soon as she felt Trisha start to shake, she chuckled. "Here," she said amid the laughter, "Let me show you the proper height to raise your arms and how to point the gun."

Trisha moved her pointer finger over the trigger.

"Wait," Clarissa ordered. "Don't pull the trigger. You're as scared as I was when I first held a gun while I was in boot camp. For now, just get comfortable holding the gun."

"Okay," Trisha sputtered, even as she struggled to grow accustomed to the heavy, metal feel of the weapon. Her hands were sweaty. She kept wiping them on her pants, as she worked to calm her nerves by taking deep breaths. The longer that she held the gun the more nauseous she felt. On top of that, the gun felt slippery, so she clutched it.

They stayed at the back of the gun shop for twenty minutes, Clarissa showing Trisha how to aim at tree limbs and tin cans. Not once did they pull the trigger. Then, Clarissa took the Ruger from Trisha and said, "Okay. You should be good. Let's get back in the car. Time to find your friends."

They drove down Highway Fifty-One for forty minutes before Clarissa switched on the right blinkers, pulled off the highway and, pressing the accelerator, sped down a narrow road.

"Where are we going?" Trisha asked, sitting up enough in the back seat to see out of the side window.

"Up and down as many side roads as we can." Peering into the rearview mirror, Clarissa asked, "Where were you when you last saw your three friends?"

"I was north of here. I think that you're going the wrong way," Trisha said, her voice barely above a whisper, the bulk of her attention on the few cabins, ranch houses and open land that they passed.

"None of this looks familiar?" Clarissa asked, frowning at the idea that Trisha was not going to reveal that she was driving in the wrong direction had she not turned off the two lane highway.

"No," Trisha shook her head and answered. "I came to your cabin from several miles to the north of where your neighbors live. As a matter of fact," she continued, "I almost stopped at your neighbor's cabin instead of yours. The only reason that I didn't was because I saw your neighbor outside, the guy you said was retired from the Navy. No way," she said, shaking her head, "was I going to approach a house that had a man in it."

"He's a good guy."

"How was I to know that? I still don't know your neighbors," she said. "And, the guy who I met at the mall in Indianapolis was nice at the start too."

"Good points," Clarissa admitted. "Good points," she repeated, pulling onto a long driveway.

"Do you know these people?" Trisha asked, crouching in the back seat.

"I'm just pulling in here so that I can turn around."

Seconds later, they were back on Highway Fifty-One. This time, when Clarissa reached the entrance to the highway, instead of turning right toward Atlanta, she turned the Camry to the left, back toward her cabin. As it had been moments earlier, the highway was mainly empty. Every several seconds, a beat up truck or an older car sped down the other side of the highway. Not once did Clarissa see a white van, a mustang or a vehicle that looked like it could store people in the back. She didn't even see a sixteen-wheeler while she sped north up Highway Fifty-One. "You're going to have to show me where you last saw your friends," Clarissa said, her gaze darting from side to side across the highway, her hands firm on the steering wheel.

"I know," Trisha said, nodding in jerky motions. "But, I was at your cabin for an entire day. I don't know where they are now. And," she added. "They took our cell phones as soon as they got us to the hotel."

"I figured that," Clarissa said, looking out across the highway. Light rain started to tap the car hood and windshield.

"Do you think that the guys went back to your cabin? You said that you saw footprints when you went outside this morning."

"Yeah. They might have gone back to the cabin," Clarissa said. "But, we're not hunting for the men. We definitely want to avoid them. But, we're trying to find the other girls."

"I hid inside a sewage drain the night before I came to your cabin," Trisha revealed.

Clarissa squinted. "There's a bridge over that way, right?"

"About half a mile away from the drain."

"Were your friends with you?"

"No," Tears pooled in Trisha's eyes. "I haven't seen them in four days." Using the back of her right hand, she swiped away the tears that went like slow rain down her face.

"We should have started looking for them as soon as you got something to eat and got a bath," Clarissa said, in hindsight. "I should have started this search earlier. That's on me," she said, peering into the mirror. She cringed as she watched Trisha wipe away tears.

The Camry ate up miles of highway.

"The guys might have caught us then," Trisha finally said. "If you saw the van the morning that I arrived at your cabin, the guys were close on my trail."

"That's true."

"They might have been back at your cabin when we returned from the search if we'd gone out looking yesterday."

"You're right," Clarissa said. Seconds later, she asked, "Can you see out the window without sitting up? We can't afford for you to be seen."

"Yes. I can see out the window." As if to prove that she could see out the car's back, side window, she told Clarissa, "I see the Chattahoochee River about a quarter mile on the right. On the left are trees and grass. It's as it was when I was on foot on the other side of the road, up that slight hill. There's hardly anything out here. I kept looking for a store, something that showed that people actually lived and hung out in this area. But, I saw next to no stores. This is not the place to be stranded or lost in," she added, leaning into the seat. She whispered, "We have to find them."

"We will find them," Clarissa said, barely believing her own words, silently begging God for help.

Four hours later, the sun hung bright in the midday sky. Not once did Clarissa or Trisha even see a kid riding a bicycle, fishing at the edge of the river or walking a dog. They did pass several jeeps, RVs and large cargo trucks. But, they didn't see a white van or a mustang.

"Do you think the guys caught them?" Trisha asked.

"I pray not," Clarissa answered.

A second later, Trisha sat up and pointed out the left side of the window. "Hey. What's that over there?"

"I don't know," Clarissa said, squinting as she looked to the left, up a dirt incline. "Looks like a raccoon," Clarissa added, steering the Camry toward the moving object. "We're more than fifty miles to the north of my cabin. Let me see if there's a road behind the highway the way there is over by my cabin. Your friends could be hiding behind a garage or a car the way that you were."

She drove the Camry off the highway up onto a dirt road. As it did by her cabin, the dirt road snaked in front of the cabins and ranch houses, winding to the right, then to the left for what appeared to be miles.

Clarissa was surprised to see how far the road went. She wasn't on the dirt road six minutes, when her gaze darted to the left. "Now, to figure out how to get behind the houses." Turning and looking over her shoulder, she asked Trisha, "How did you get behind the cabins?"

"I was on foot."

"So, you just cut across the yards?"

"There was a split in the road behind the houses not too far from here," Trisha said, sitting so close to the front seat that her breath blew the hair on the nape of Clarissa's neck up.

"Okay," Clarissa sighed, growing tired of driving. "Let's keep looking on both sides of the road. The girls probably aren't hiding out on the highway," she said. "It would be too easy to see them if they were running down the highway." A second later, she said, "You know what?" She didn't wait for Trisha to respond. "You tell me where you'd go if you were still trying to escape on foot."

Their search led them another ten miles down the road to where the road ended. Then, they drove back onto the highway.

Clarissa pulled over onto the highway shoulder and checked her WAZE app on her cell phone. "It's more than two hundred miles to my townhouse," she moaned.

"I'm too tired to do that today, especially after we search for the girls for at least a couple more hours."

She searched the WAZE app again. "What do you say we go get some gas and then head toward Atlanta again?" She paused. "Show me where you started running four days ago, the place where you escaped from. We have to be close to the place."

"I don't want to go back there," Trisha begged.

"No. We're just going to drive by."

"Why?"

"So, I can turn around in the car and go back over the path that you all took. And," Clarissa asked. "How did you all get separated?"

"We decided that it was best to take off running in different directions as soon as we escaped."

"That's right," Clarissa said. "You did say that yesterday."

Their drive led them to a truck stop. "Another empty truck stop," Clarissa said. It surprised her to see Trisha already laying across the back seat covered beneath the blanket.

Clarissa didn't go inside the truck stop. Instead, she swiped her debit card at the pump, then filled the Camry with gas.

"Gotta go to the bathroom?" she asked Trisha after she opened the driver side door.

"Not here," Trisha said, refusing to sit up.

"Is this the place?" Clarissa asked, standing and looking toward the building about sixty yards from the pump.

"Ye-Yes," Trisha stuttered. "Get out of here," she screamed.

Clarissa reached inside the car for her Glock. "Stay in the car," she told Trisha. "I'm going to walk around the place."

"Drive around," Trisha told her.

"Stay here," Clarissa advised. "I'm locking the car doors and going inside. I'm also going to set the alarm on the car. No one will bother you."

"Don't go in there," Trisha begged. "Don't leave me," she pleaded, the volume in her voice rising.

From where she stood at the edge of the passenger door, Clarissa could see that Trisha's body was shaking. "Calm down," she told Trisha. "You have to calm yourself and stop shaking. We won't be here long."

"No," Trisha wept. "Don't go in there."

"Stay here. Keep the door locked. Stay under the blanket and pull your feet up. You'll be safe in the car," Clarissa assured her. "I'll be right back."

Next, Clarissa put the Glock in the front waistband of her blue jeans. Then, she walked to the far left side of the building. She walked all the way to the building's back edge. Seeing nothing except two large dumpsters, she returned to the front of the building. Then, she entered the building and looked around. She hunted for any young girl's face. Seeing none, she grabbed two bottled waters, paid for the water and returned to the Camry.

"Just one cashier in the building," she told Trisha. "And, here," she said, handing Trisha a bottled water. "I got both of us one. These are cooler than the ones in the bag that I packed before we left the cabin."

"They drop girls off at truck stops, so men can pay to have sex with them," she told Clarissa after she took the water.

"No one was in there except for the cashier," Clarissa said. "At least I didn't see anyone else. Let's head back toward Atlanta and keep looking for the girls down that way." She paused. "When you all broke up and went your separate ways, did any of the girls head north?"

"No. We all headed south, toward the Chattahoochee River. But, I turned back after awhile, toward where your cabin is. I stayed close to the river though. Right from the start, we all were prepared to hide in the river if we had to. It's a good way not to get caught. It's hard to see deep into a river at night."

Clarissa pulled to the edge of the parking lot. Then, she put the car in reverse.

"What are you doing?" Trisha screamed.

"Taking pictures of this shit hole with my cell phone so we have pictures to turn into some decent cops."

"Don't go back in," Trisha begged. "Don't you leave me again. Don't you dare. I hate this place," Trisha screamed. "Get me out of here."

"We're leaving," Clarissa said, snapping four pictures of the truck stop, one with the location's street number on the top of the building. Dropping her cell phone inside the Camry's cup tray, she sped out onto the highway, dirt and gravel swirling up behind the Camry.

****

They stopped for gas one more time. Then, night descended, cloaking the area in darkness. Clarissa had to squint to see the road good. When she drove around tight curves on the highway, she switched on her high beams so that she could see.

Crickets, great horned owls and bull frogs filled the area with noise. "We're going to have to head back to the cabin," Clarissa said. "We've driven a few hundred miles south of the cabin that I'm renting and at least another two-hundred and fifty miles back toward my cabin, not to mention driving down I-don't-know-how-many backroads. I have the place for another week, so we're good. I was going to turn around and drive south again back to my permanent townhouse. But, I'm too tired to keep driving tonight."

As soon as they drove down the dirt road toward her cabin, the Camry's high beams on, Clarissa saw another, larger break in her basement window. "Not again," she moaned.

She parked the Camry in the driveway. "Come with me," she told Trisha, pulling out her gun. She headed for the back porch.

"Stay behind me," she told Trisha.

Her gun was drawn as she made her way through the back door which she immediately locked. Then, she stole her way into the kitchen and living room. Next, she went upstairs and checked each of the bedrooms, the upstairs office, the attic, the bathrooms and closets. The last place that she checked was the basement. "I don't have anymore plywood," she said, when she turned and looked at Trisha. "Guess I'll have to put more plastic up to the window," she added. "Please hand me that roll of masking tape."

They worked quickly. It didn't take them ten minutes to cover the new break in the window with thick plastic.

Clarissa's lips were pursed when she turned. "Gotta get more plywood. Can't afford to let the basement flood. Because I'm only renting this cabin, I could be responsible for repairs should it rain and the basement get flooded."

They climbed the basement stairs and headed into the living room.

"I have to go to the bathroom bad," Trisha said, clutching her stomach at the edge of the living room.

"Sure," Clarissa said. "Go ahead."

Five minutes later, Clarissa leaped off the sofa when she heard sirens blaring. Absent forethought, she yanked the front door open. Her mouth flew ajar. It shocked her to see two police cars, their lights flashing and spinning.

The police cars were parked in front of her neighbor's cabin. "Trisha, go in the guest bedroom and lock the door," she said after she closed the front door.

"What's going on?" Trisha asked, zipping her pants and flushing the toilet. She ran back downstairs. Stepping alongside Clarissa, she peered through the living room blinds.

"I don't know," Clarissa said. "Mark and Lois live such quiet lives. They're kids are grown, living out west in California. Can't imagine why the cops would be at their house." Turning, she grabbed her book bag and pulled out her Glock. "But I'm about to find out."

"Can't I just stay down here?" Trisha asked. "Do I have to lock myself in the guest bedroom? I won't let anyone in and I damn sure won't go out."

"No," Clarissa said, shaking her head. "I don't know what's going on." She shook her head again. "Can't risk someone seeing your outline from the porch or road." She looked into Trisha's eyes, their bottom lids drooping, sad. "We cannot afford to lose a step. We can't afford to get lazy or take anything for granted." Placing her hands against the sides of Trisha's shoulders, she looked into Trisha's eyes and said, "I am not willing to let any harm come to you or to me." She worked at a smile. "We have got to stay sharp. As much as we want this to be over, we simply cannot afford to think that everything is fine."

"Okay," Trisha nodded. Then, she turned and headed up the stairs to the guest bedroom.

"Keep the light off and stay away from the window."

"Do you still have the other gun?" Trisha asked from the top of the stairs.

"You won't need it," Clarissa told her, not yet comfortable leaving Trisha alone with a gun. She climbed the stairs. "There's a baseball bat in the guest bedroom," she told Trisha as soon as she entered the guest bedroom. "It's right here," she added, reaching into the closet. "You can keep the bat right here next to you on the bed."

"Is it okay if I turn the television on?" Trisha asked, turning toward the flat screen television hanging from the wall across from the bed that she sat on.

"Not now. I don't want anything to distract you should anyone stop by the house while I'm away. I'm not expecting anyone to come here," she was quick to add. "However, if anyone does come here, you are to stay in this room with the door locked. Don't make a sound. I'll be outside by Mark's and Lois'. I'll keep watch on the cabin. But, I can only see the front of the cabin from Mark's and Lois'."

"Okay," Trisha said, gazing into her lap.

"I'll be back in five to ten minutes. My goal is to get back here as soon as possible."

"Okay," Trisha nodded, peering up at Clarissa.

Clarissa hurried out of the bedroom then downstairs. She turned the cabin alarm on as soon as she locked the front door. Then, she ran up the dirt road to Mark's and Lois' cabin.

Lois was the first person who Clarissa saw. She stood at the front of the first police car with her arms crossed, wearing a pair of croc jean shorts and a short-sleeved, cotton blouse.

"What's going on?" Clarissa asked, nearing Lois' side.

"A girl broke into our basement," Lois said, pulling loose strands of her red hair behind her ears. "Don't know how she got in there," Lois said, shaking her head. "She broke the window. That much we know. But, how she broke the thick basement window, I-I-I don't know. That window is too thick to break with a rock."

"She must have been scared, terrified to try to break in like that," Clarissa said. She started walking toward the first police cruiser. "Where is the girl? Is she in the police car?"

"Yes," Lois said. "Mark's in the basement with the other cop."

Clarissa walked to the side of the police cruiser. She looked at the girl, noticing how the girl was about the same age as Trisha. Yet, she didn't want to tell Lois or Mark about Trisha. She had come to feel responsible for Trisha's safety. Based on what Clarissa knew about sex slave trafficking, she figured that keeping Trisha a secret was best.

Clarissa knocked on the police car's back window.

The girl looked at her.

"Are you okay?" she mouthed to the girl.

"No," the girl mouthed back.

Turning away from the car, Clarissa asked Lois, "Where's the cop who drove this car?"

"He must have gone into the basement with Mark and the other cop," Lois said. Her brows went up. "He was right here a few seconds ago."

"Is it okay if I go down by the basement?"

"Sure," Lois said. "I'll go with you. I don't know what's taking them so long anyway."

"Well," Clarissa said, "I think that one of us should stay here with the girl. Maybe you can ask the guys what's taking so long. I'll stay here with the girl."

Lois peered at Clarissa with a raised brow. "Sure," she said. Seconds later, Lois was gone around the side of Mark's and her cabin, toward their basement window.

Lois gone, Clarissa returned her attention to the girl. "What's your name?" she asked, knocking on the car window.

The girl, her brown eyes wide, her healthy, wooly hair pulled back into a thick shoulder-length ponytail, rolled the window down. "What?"

"I asked, what's your name?" Clarissa smiled, hoping to quell the girl's fears.

"My name's Amber."

"Amber. Amber," Clarissa heard herself ponder. The name repeating loud like a banging drum in her head, she stood stunned in silence. One end of her blouse hung down off her shoulder, yet she didn't move. It was as if she had become a mannequin. And, her feet

felt stuck, heavy. She starred at Amber for a long time, wondering if her day long search had happened upon its great find, an indescribable pearl. Finally, she leaned close to the window and asked, "Do you know Trisha?"

Amber's eyes ballooned. Then, they darted, as if searching for an answer. Her lips trembled, parted ever so slightly, formed a small 'o', but she didn't speak.

"You do," Clarissa stepped back and said. She lowered her arms then spread her hands as if preparing for a surprise. "You all ran away four days ago with Jackie and Wanda, right?"

Amber nodded, her dirty fingers toying with the top edge of the wide strap, pink dress that she wore. Then, she asked, "How do you know about Trisha, Jackie and Wanda?"

"Trisha's been rescued," she told her.

Amber's gaze lowered as she digested the information. She sat with her legs close together; her knees touched.

"My name's Clarissa. I used to be in the Navy. I've been renting the cabin next door." Reaching into her pant pocket, she pulled out her wallet. "Here's my driver license."

Amber looked hard at the license after she took it from Clarissa.

And," Clarissa added, digging further inside her wallet. "Here's my passport."

Placing the driver license and passport side by side, Amber looked at the picture on the license and the picture on the passport. She took note of Clarissa's wide forehead, braids and broad smile. Then, she glanced up at Clarissa, and, returning the driver license and passport to Clarissa, she nodded.

"I'm going to get you out of here," Clarissa told her. "Let me go talk with the cops. I'll tell them that I know you, that you're my niece and that you ran away this morning and are coming back with me. Okay?" she said, seeking a sign from Amber that she agreed with the plan.

"Where's Trisha?"

Clarissa thought fast. She reached into her pant pocket and retrieved her cell phone. Flipping through her phone's camera gallery, she gasped when she spotted a picture of the truck stop that included the side of Trisha's face in the upper right corner. "Here," Clarissa said, holding the phone up so that Amber could see it.

"Trisha's safe," Clarissa told her. "I know it's a risk, going with me. But, if you stay here with the cops, you could end up in a bad foster care situation until you get reconnected with your family, and that's if the cops aren't crooked. If the cops are crooked," she said, glancing over her shoulder at Lois' and Mark's cabin, "You could end up right back where you just ran from."

"Why should I trust you?"

"Because this whole scene just fell into my lap," Clarissa lowered her voice and said. She leaned close to the car window. "I didn't ask for this. Trisha showed up at my cabin out-of-the-blue. She was hiding next to my car in the driveway."

Amber stared at Clarissa, her head titled upward, her gaze fixed on Clarissa's top brow.

"You should trust me because I can get you home safely without the risk of you being captured or sold into another trafficking outfit, without you becoming part of the state system."

"Okay," Amber acquiesced, eyeballing Lois, Mark and the cops as they started to move away from the cabin's basement window. She couldn't get the picture of Trisha out of her head.

Clarissa didn't take two steps from the car when she turned back. Leaning close to the window, she whispered, "My sister's name is April Bloomfield. She and her husband, Chris, live in Cincinnati, Ohio. Remember. You're their daughter who ran away. Your name is Amber Bloomfield."

"Okay," Amber nodded.

"Wait here," Clarissa said as she tapped the car door.

"Okay," Amber agreed, praying that she was making the right decision, anxious to see Trisha again.

"I know that girl," Clarissa told the cops as she approached the corner of Lois' and Mark's cabin. "I've been looking for her. She's my niece Amber," Clarissa said, searching Lois' and Mark's faces, hoping that they believed her.

"Clarissa, is she the daughter of your sister who lives in Ohio?" Lois asked.

"Lois, that's not important right now," Mark said, walking around the two police officers toward Clarissa. "The important thing is that the girl has been found and that she's safe."

The cops eyeballed Clarissa. "I can call my sister, April. She lives in Cincinnati, Ohio. She'll confirm it,"

Clarissa said. "My sister called this morning after I left the cabin to go sightseeing. She thought my niece would fly here. But, I didn't believe her." She shook her head. "I didn't think she'd bolt like that and fly here. She's never done it before." She looked right at the cops. "My niece and I are close. She and her mother had a fight," Clarissa said, shaking her head. "I know my niece regrets leaving home and my sister is worried sick." Glancing at the cops, she added, "I'm so glad you found her."

"Let's go talk with the girl," the taller cop said.

They all walked away from the window and headed back toward the first police car.

"I'll pay for the damages," Clarissa said, turning and looking over her shoulder at Lois and Mark.

"That's okay," Mark waved. "We're just happy that your niece is fine."

"Do you know this woman?" the taller cop asked Amber after he opened the police car's back door.

"Yes," Amber nodded, the photo that Clarissa had showed her of Trisha top of her mind. "She's my aunt Clarissa."

"Here's my driver license and passport," Clarissa told the taller cop.

"Run the license," he told his partner. "It's procedure," he told Clarissa.

"I understand," Clarissa nodded. She watched the shorter cop walk to the other police cruiser, her license and passport in hand.

Moments later, the cop returned and told the taller cop, "She's clean."

After they lobbed several rounds of questions at Amber and Clarissa, the cops released Amber into Clarissa's custody. "Thank you," Clarissa nodded, holding Amber close to her chest. "Thank you," she repeated, this time looking toward Mark and Lois.

Clarissa, Amber, Lois and Mark stood outside and watched the cop cars pull away from the cabin and drive south down the dirt road toward the highway.

"Thank you," Clarissa told Lois and Mark, the cops gone. "Let me get my purse so that I can pay you for the broken window."

"No," Mark told Clarissa. "Keep the money. Just take care of your niece." He winked when he looked at Clarissa, signaling to her that he knew that Amber wasn't her niece.

A second later, Mark had a sobering thought. "Clarissa?" he asked, "What's going on? Are you okay?"

"I've got to get her to safety," Clarissa said, looking from Mark to Lois. "She was just trying to find a place to hide, a place to be safe."

Lois looked at Amber, who stood so close to Clarissa, it looked like she was trying to merge with Clarissa in effort to hide.

"If anyone, and I mean anyone, should come here looking for any girls, please-please tell them that you haven't seen anyone," Clarissa begged.

"Are you safe?" Lois asked Clarissa.

"Yes," Clarissa said. "I just have to get her out of here. I want to get her to my townhouse. Then, I've got to get her on a plane home."

"Clarissa," Mark said, "You've mentioned a van. Plus, some guys stopped by our cabin the other night asking if we'd seen teenage girls. Was she kidnapped?"

Lois looked at Mark, fear in her eyes. Then, she looked at Clarissa.

"Yes," Clarissa admitted.

"Okay," Mark nodded. "You don't have to say anything else. I know what to do," he told her. "We'll cover your tracks if anyone comes by."

"Thank you," Clarissa said. "Thank you." Then, she turned and walked back down the road to her cabin, Amber at her side.

"Go on in," Clarissa said as soon as they entered her cabin through the back door. "I'm just going to lock the door."

Amber went one slow step after another inside the cabin. Once inside, she stood with her hands penned behind her back. She didn't utter a word. Instead, she stared across the kitchen at the hand-clock above the stove.

"Come on," Clarissa said, biding Amber to follow her. "We're not going to be down here long," she said, looking over her shoulder at Amber as they descended the basement steps.

The heavy clunk noise that Amber's right foot made when it landed against a stair hinted at a leg injury.

"Did you hurt your leg while you were outside?" Clarissa asked after they reached the basement floor.

"I think so." She jerked her calf back when Clarissa leaned over and extended her hand to examine the injury.

"We'll get you fixed up once we get upstairs," Clarissa assured her. Then, she turned and hunted for the box of drinking glasses that she'd seen in the basement the first day that she had arrived at the cabin. They were on top of two other boxes that were filled with blankets and towels. The boxes were the few items at the cabin that signaled to Clarissa that someone other than she ever stayed at the cabin.

Rising on her toes, Clarissa opened the top box and started pulling out drinking glasses, unwrapping them from the protective newspaper that they were covered in. Then, she placed the glasses on the floor beneath the window. Next, she crossed the floor and retrieved a box of razor blades off the shelf above the washing machine.

Amber didn't budge. She stood with her heels pushed against the bottom basement step, her hands again penned behind her back.

Clarissa opened the box that the razor blades were in and shook the blades across the floor beneath the window. Then, she stopped, turning and looking at Amber. "Did you try to come in here earlier? Did you break my window too?"

"Ye-Yes," Amber stuttered.

"It's okay," Clarissa smiled. "The important thing is that you're safe."

Razor blades sprinkling the floor, spread among the drinking glasses, Clarissa walked to the other side of the basement. She returned the empty razor blade box to the top shelf. When she neared the basement steps again, she asked Amber, "Was someone chasing you while you were out here?"

As hard as she worked to conceal her fears from Amber and Trisha, just knowing that the men who were looking for the girls had been in the area left Clarissa no room for comfort. It terrified her that they could all be caught and forced into sex slavery.

When Amber didn't answer, Clarissa stared at her and repeated, " Was someone chasing you while you were out here?"

"No."

"Good," Clarissa said. "I put those glasses and razor blades by the window so they'll create noise and cut whoever might try to get in here. But," she added, "Let's hope it doesn't come to that." After a pause, she looked at Amber and said, "Come on. Let's go back upstairs."

Once inside the kitchen, Clarissa placed a chair in front of the back door and in front of the basement door. She did the same to the front door when they entered the living room. Then, she led Amber upstairs.

Amber moved cautiously all the way up the steps. She braced herself by placing her hands on the stairwell wall, as if she was moving through pitch blackness, as if she was afraid that she'd fall. Her caution remained spiked after she reached the second floor, until she rounded the corner. She saw Trisha's smooth mocha colored skin, her arched eyebrows, her long flat forehead and her wide-pudgy nose before she actually realized who she was looking at. For just a second, she paused, hanging in the realm of disbelief, and looked intently at the girl staring back at her.

Then, the reality of what was occurring sunk in and, like a sailfish charging away from shore, Amber bolted away from Clarissa and ran toward Trisha. The two girls rocked inside one another's arms, hugging each other and weeping. They stayed that way for a long time. It was as if they were born together, birthed inside the other's embrace.

Clarissa cried openly, not once bothering to swipe at her tears with the back of her hand, while she stood at the bedroom door's edge. "First thing tomorrow morning, we head to Atlanta," she blubbered. "In the meantime, Trisha, you can show Amber where the bathroom is. Amber, I'll get you clothes to wear to bed tonight after you shower or enjoy a bubble bath. I'll also give you clothes to put on tomorrow morning. We have to be ready to go before the sun comes up."

Chapter Eight

At four o'clock the following morning, the neighborhood dark and the moon hanging like a white, cloudy balloon in the sky, Clarissa, Amber and Trisha moved through the cabin with haste. Trisha and Amber leaned over the guest bedroom's double sink brushing their teeth so fast that their toothbrushes almost slipped out of their hands and fell down the drain.

"Dress quickly," Clarissa said from where she stood at the bathroom doorway. "Lois sent me a text saying that she saw two men snooping around their cabin. We have to get out of here right now."

When Trisha turned, her mouth frothy with toothpaste, Clarissa was gone. "You sure you didn't leave a piece of clothing or a string behind to remember your way, so you wouldn't get lost if you had to turn and run in another direction while you were out in the woods?"

"No, Trisha," Amber said. She rinsed her mouth out with a cup of lukewarm water. Then, she wiped her mouth dry with the back of her hand. "I told you, I was careful the whole time before Clarissa's neighbors called the cops after I busted their basement window. I didn't leave anything."

"I'm not saying you did," Trisha said, wiping her mouth on the hand towel hanging on the rack. She left the bathroom and walked into the bedroom. "It's just that--" Pausing, Trisha pulled the long t-shirt that she'd worn as her pajamas over her head and shoved the t-shirt in a plastic bag. Then, she stepped into a pair of jeans.

"It's just what?" Amber asked, turning off the bathroom light and following Trisha inside the bedroom.

"It's just that I tore off strips of my dress and tied them to a few trees so I wouldn't get lost if the guys came running after me," she confessed. "I was so scared of getting caught. I was so scared of getting lost in the woods."

"Don't feel bad," Amber told her while she pulled on a yellow cotton blouse that Clarissa had laid across the bed for her. "I was scared to death of getting caught myself. I even got chased by a coyote one night. I ended up sleeping in a tree."

"That's another reason I stayed close to the river," Trisha said. She pulled on the purple cotton blouse that Clarissa laid out for her. "I figured hiding in water would wash away my scent so coyotes, bobcats and foxes wouldn't spot me."

"Can you believe we made it?" Amber asked, her lips quivering. "We made it. We got this far."

"I'm not going back," Trisha told her. Shaking her head, she added, "If the guys find us, I'll do something desperate. I'll-I'll do anything. I'll do something crazy not to get caught. I don't care what it cost me. I'm not going back."

While Amber and Trisha talked, Clarissa crawled on her hands and knees across the living room floor. Similar to a long-armed cat, she swiped her left arm and hand beneath the living room sofa and chairs, feeling for a note, a receipt, any slip of paper that could reveal her, Trisha's or Amber's identities.

Feeling nothing, she stood and moved the furniture away from the walls. Then, she went back to her knees and hands and swiped beneath the furniture a second time.

She did the same in the kitchen and basement. While she was in the basement, she also grabbed the broom that lay against a wall close to the washing machine. She picked up the glasses and returned them to the box on the shelf. Then, she took the broom and swept up the razor blades, eager to leave no sign that she'd been at the cabin. It took four trips to the garbage bin that was placed on the left side of the washing machine for Clarissa to clean the floor. The floor clean, she continued her inspection of the basement.

At the far left edge of the basement, her hands shook when she came across Amber's spring dress. It had fallen between the washer and dryer. She used the end of the broom to push at the dress, bringing it to the washing machine's front edge.

Pulling the dress close to her chest, she squeezed it and shuddered. Then, she ran up the stairs and told Amber and Trisha, "Not a trace. Don't leave a trace. It's got to be like we don't exist."

Amber gasped when Clarissa tossed her spring dress across the top of the plastic bag that Clarissa had given her last night to put the rest of her clothes in. Stepping back, she said, "The dress must have fell when I was folding my underwear after I washed them late last night." Sighing, she said, "I should have just washed my clothes in the bathroom sink."

"No. It's fine," Clarissa told her, softening her stance. "I double checked everything." She turned over her wrist and looked at her digital watch. "You two ready? We have to be out of here in less than three minutes."

"Did the lady next door text you again?" Trisha asked, grabbing the plastic bag that she'd shoved her extra set of clothes in and heading toward the bedroom door.

"No. And, I don't want to bother them. It's so early. When I checked the security cameras a few minutes ago, everything was clear. All three of us are leaving this cabin together right now, and we're going to be hustling."

"Okay," Amber said. She looked at the brush that Clarissa had let her borrow. It lay across the edge of the dresser.

"Bring everything that has your hair in it, everything that has your scent on it, everything," Clarissa ordered. "If the guys did come back here and were snooping around Lois' and Mark's, they may be on to us. We cannot risk anything. And, we've got to get the hell out of here now."

Shoving the brush in her plastic bag, Amber turned back and gave the bedroom one final look over. Then, she followed Trisha and Clarissa downstairs.

They ran all the way to the back door. Then, Clarissa said, "Stay here." She checked the security cameras one last time. Next, she took down the extra security cameras that she'd put up, shoved them in her book bag and headed for the back door again.

"Let me go first," she told Trisha and Amber, moving around the side of the girls then in front of them.

She took in a deep breath and turned the back door lock. It was pitch black outside. As soon as Clarissa stepped off the first porch step, a chipmunk darted across the driveway, toward the back of the cabin.

Just as it did, Clarissa fell back. She almost screamed. But, instead she placed her hand against her chest and pressed down. Her heart felt like it was beating too fast.

Hurrying to the driver side, she pressed the door locks open and told Amber and Trisha to, "Come on. Run."

After they ran to the car and slid across the back seat, Clarissa sprinted up the cabin's back steps and locked the door. Then, she ran back to the car and sat behind the steering wheel.

"All right," she said as she adjusted the rearview mirror. Her book bag was on the passenger seat, heavy with her Glock. Amber and Trisha sat scrunched down in the back seat. They each wore jeans and a short-sleeved cotton blouse. Anyone passing the Camry would have believed that Clarissa was alone in the car. "Let's find Jackie and Wanda and get you all home. But, first, we have to stop by my townhouse. It's near Atlanta, which is where we'll search for Jackie and Wanda." She nodded into, "Mark and Lois will let me know if they see any teen girls looking out of place around the cabin area. But," she shook her head and added, "Something tells me that Jackie and Wanda are near Atlanta. It's a big city. I'd head for a big city if I was on foot and seeking safety. Plus, you said Jackie is from Atlanta. It's a lot closer than Philly.

Maybe Jackie and Wanda paired up and tried to get to Jackie's family's house."

"Stopping by your townhouse is going to cost us time," Amber said.

"No," Clarissa said. "If Jackie headed home and that's certainly what I'd do, it'll put us a lot closer to her. My townhouse is less than ten miles from Atlanta. Plus, we're going to look for Jackie and Wanda while we drive to my townhouse."

"Okay," Amber sighed, resigning herself into making another trip that she hadn't asked for.

In front of them, Clarissa pressed her right foot on the accelerator and pulled out of the driveway. Then, she sped down the dirt road toward Highway Fifty-One. A smile tugged at her mouth when she thought about Mark and Lois and how helpful they might become at throwing the men off the girls' trail. Seconds later, she worried about what could happen if the guys got dicey and managed to overtake Lois should she venture outdoors alone at the wrong time.

She banged her fist on the steering wheel and cursed, "Damn! A woman isn't safe anywhere in this world." Then, she pressed the brake, stopped the Camry and just breathed. Images of Lois being snatched from the edge of Mark and her front lawn troubled her, growing in clarity with each deep breath that she inhaled.

As hard as she tried to calm her thoughts, she couldn't rid her mind of the images.

Five deep breaths in, she punched the accelerator again. "Where do you think the other girls are, Amber?" She glanced into the rearview mirror, her gaze catching the final, small outline of Mark's and Lois' cabin, now a distant shadow. At the same time, she turned on the windshield wipers, rain starting to fall lightly out of the sky.

"I don't know. I kept looking for Jackie and Wanda while I was searching for a place to hide out overnight. But, I didn't see them."

"When's the last time you saw them?" Trisha asked Amber.

"The last time I saw Jackie and Wanda was when we all ran away and decided that it was best that we take off in different directions." She paused. "Do you really think that was a good idea?"

"Remember. We thought we'd get caught if we stuck together." Trisha shrugged. "It was better that one of us got free, went to a women's shelter or FBI office and reported the men. We know places that the guys work. We know what they look like. We could get them arrested."

"Sounds like you all had a good plan," Clarissa interjected. "It is better that at least one of you get completely free," she said. "And, we are definitely going to report those men."

Rain tapped the Camry's hood faster. Heavy rain drops flowed down the windshield. Clarissa flipped the wipers to "fast". The wipers swung from the left to the right so fast that they made a dull click sound as they swooshed back and forth. "How did you both end up in the same area out by the cabins?" Clarissa wanted to know.

"I followed the Chattahoochee River," Amber said. "I figured that was the safest thing to do. I could just jump into the river if I needed to hide, especially at night."

"That's what I did too," Trisha said.

"But, how did you know that the Chattahoochee River was even in this area?" Clarissa asked.

"We'd been planning an escape almost since we got caught," Amber said.

"Yes," Trisha chimed. "We never planned on staying. Every chance we could, we looked around. We asked customers questions when the guys took us to convenience stores."

"People at truck stop convenience stores," Amber said.

"Over nighters at restaurants and hotels too," Trisha added.

"Well," Clarissa said, leaning forward and squinting through the falling rain. "One of you keep your gaze fixed on the side of the highway that's closest to the river. The other one stay focused on the other side of the road. Right now, I'm focused on getting you to my townhouse in Sandy Springs. Oh, and, Amber?"

"Yes?"

"Do you have a cell phone? Trisha told me that the guys took your phones when you all first met up. But, I didn't know if you had a chance to get another cell phone since you escaped."

"No. I never saw a store to buy a cell phone from while I was running. I did try to get a prepaid phone almost as soon as we were kidnapped. The first time, we were at a truck stop. I had just been with this filthy fortyish executive. He stank. He was disgusting and he kept talking to me like he owned me. While we were at the truck stop convenience store, one of the guys spotted me eyeballing the cell phones and threatened to kill me if I got a phone. I still kept some money after each paid-for-rape. I'd coax the pigs who slept with me to give me extra money. I used that money to buy food." She dug her hand in her right blue jeans pocket. "I've got two hundred dollars left. If your neighbors hadn't called the cops on me, I was going to get to the nearest airport and catch a flight home." She stared at the clump of crumbled twenty dollar bills. "That was always my plan."

"You know what?" Clarissa said, pulling onto the highway's shoulder. Her tires spun when they splashed over a row of puddles. "Why don't you both search my laptop to see if you can locate the area where you think Jackie and Wanda may have headed? I connected my phone to my laptop months ago. I'll find a hot spot and you can start searching." Before the girls could respond, Clarissa was outside the car in the pouring rain digging through the trunk for her laptop.

"Here," she said, climbing back onto the driver seat, her hair, shoulders and back wet. She handed Trisha her laptop. "I found a hotspot. The battery should last until we get to my townhouse."

"Do you live close to here?" Amber asked.

"We're a good ways away from where I live," Clarissa told her.

They spent the next five hours searching alleyways, side roads, gas stations and three truck stops. Clarissa even pulled the Camry into a dozen private residential driveways and asked homeowners if they'd seen two young girls walking alone. Each effort turned up empty, left Clarissa physically drained and Trisha and Amber more emotionally traumatized and frightened.

Fatigue had settled upon each of them by the time Clarissa pulled inside a grocery store parking lot at the edge of Sandy Springs. "Come on," she said. "We won't be in here long. Just want to grab some veggies, eggs, fruit and a few other items."

As soon as they returned to the Camry, Trisha and Amber resumed their online search for places where Jackie and Wanda might have gone. They weren't far from the grocery store when Trisha pointed at the laptop screen and hollered, "They may have gone to this hotel. An older woman there knew something wasn't right when we came to the hotel with two of the guys. On our way out of the hotel, she pulled us to the side and told us to contact her if we ever needed anything." Turning to Amber, she smiled faintly and said, "Remember, Amber?"

"Yes," Amber nodded, her face drawn down. No sight of Jackie or Wanda after searching for them for five hours had forced her to face the fear that she might never see Jackie or Wanda again. She sat with her hands folded in her lap. She'd been sitting that way for a long time.

"You okay, Amber?" Trisha asked, her hand resting on the laptop, the image of the vintage Androssa Hotel pulled up on the screen. Both Amber and she continued to sit scrunched down in the back seat.

"Okay, you two, we're finally at my townhouse," Clarissa shared. She glanced into the rearview mirror at Amber who had gone stoic. "We'll head for the Androssa Hotel after we get settled. Just because we didn't see the girls while we searched for them on the drive to my townhouse, doesn't mean that we're giving up. Oh, no," she added, shaking her head, "We're not going to stop looking for Jackie and Wanda."

The rain had stopped. Sunrays poured through the Camry's windows. The car bumped up the asphalt entrance then pulled inside the guest parking lot area at the gated townhouse community that Clarissa lived in. A circle of tulips, roses and daisies decorated the area with a burst of color. The flowers were rooted in the grassy dirt mount that surrounded the "Welcome to Avonton Ridge" sign just outside the rental office and clubhouse. Inside the community clubhouse was a pool table, two huge flat screen televisions, a seating area, an office center, kitchenette, gym and a mail center.

To the right of the clubhouse was a swimming pool. The pool was surrounded by a twenty-foot red, metal gate.

Clarissa pressed her small black security device, the one dangling on her keychain, and the community's black steel vehicle entrance gate swung open. When the white security bar behind the gate raised, Clarissa drove up a slight hill where there were two blocks of townhouses. Taking the second left, she drove behind several townhouses, each adorned with a front porch large enough for four chairs and a small round table to fill. She stopped near the end of the row of townhouses.

"We're here," Clarissa said, pulling inside the garage next to her townhouse. It was a two-level townhouse with beige siding on the second level and red brick on the outer first level.

Amber and Trisha sat up and glanced at each other, searching one another for comfort. Trisha exited the Camry first. Then, Amber opened the left back passenger door and stepped outside. At once, she grabbed and massaged her lower back. Then, she stood and looked at Trisha. Both girls stared at the townhouses, cars and garages behind Clarissa's home. They welcomed the cool breezes that blew across their shoulders and the sides of their faces.

"You have your own yard," Trisha finally said, turning and looking over her shoulder, making sure that no one was watching them, following them.

"Yes," Clarissa smiled. She tossed her book bag over her shoulder and grabbed her suitcase out of the trunk. Then, she peered inside the back window and checked to ensure that Amber and Trisha had gotten everything off the back seat. "The yard is a little bit of earth. My paternal grandmother had a large, flourishing garden. She grew tulips, marigolds, carnations and petunias at the front and back of the home that she and my grandfather lived in for more than fifty years."

Trisha peered across the sky as if recalling a memory. "My mom keeps a garden at our house in Indianapolis." Biting back tears, she added, "She does a good job with that garden."

"My grandmother keeps a garden too," Amber said. "My mom doesn't. She's way too busy working two jobs as a nurse and department store cashier to keep a garden. It wouldn't have nothing but weeds in it if she did start one."

"You're going to get back to them," Clarissa said as she hoisted her suitcase onto the porch. "You'll get back to your families if I have to drive you home myself. But, first," she said, unlocking the townhouse's front door. "We have to find Jackie and Wanda. That's the job for the rest of the night." Using the end of her foot, she pushed the suitcase inside the foyer. "We have to search the Internet like mad until we figure out where Jackie and Wanda might be. And, we're definitely going to that hotel."

Trisha and Amber followed Clarissa inside her house. They held tight to the plastic bags that contained their spring dresses and extra pair of underwear.

"Come on," Clarissa said when she turned and saw Trisha and Amber still standing in the foyer. "It's safe. The only pet that I have is my pet turtle, Ralphael," she smiled. "There are no dogs to worry about."

After Amber and Trisha stepped from the foyer into the living room, Clarissa hurried and locked the front door. Then, she waved her hand over her shoulder and told Trisha and Amber to, "Follow me."

She walked the girls through the entire first level, showing them the dining room, kitchen and living room. Next, she took them upstairs and pointed out the bathrooms and the two guest bedrooms. "You can put your bags on a bed in one of the guest bedrooms," she told them. "For now, let's go back downstairs. I want to treat you both to one of my famous veggie and cheese omelets. Then," she added, exhaling so hard that the front edges of her hair blew up, "I have to sit down. I'm exhausted."

Ever mindful to keep Trisha and Amber relaxed, Clarissa kept talking as they descended the living room stairs. "When we get back in the kitchen, you can search for more places where you think Jackie and Wanda might be."

They weren't in the kitchen two minutes when Clarissa turned and ran back upstairs. When she returned to the kitchen, she was carrying another laptop and a pen and notepad. "Time isn't on our side," she said. "While you all search for places where you think Wanda and Jackie might be on the first laptop, after I cook us each an omelet, I'm going to search for women's shelters and sex slave trafficking support organizations on this second laptop."

As she'd always done, Clarissa scrambled the eggs in a large skillet that she lightly greased with extra virgin olive oil. Then, she diced tomatoes, an onion, mushrooms and spinach and tossed the vegetables over the cooking eggs. She sprinkled the vegetables with two cups of shredded mild cheddar cheese.

"Pomegranate juice okay?" Clarissa asked Trisha and Amber as she turned the stove off and removed the skillet from the front to the back, right burner.

"That's fine." Trisha stood and looked at the cupboard. "Where are the plates?"

"And where's the silverware and glasses?" Amber stood and asked.

"Silverware's in this small drawer right next to the stove." Pointing at the top cupboard just above the dish washer, Clarissa said, "Glasses and plates are in that cupboard."

After the girls set the table, Clarissa folded the omelet with a metal spatula. Then, she cut the egg in three triangle shapes and served them each a slice.

Trisha poured the pomegranate juice and they all sat.

"Let's say grace," Clarissa encouraged. She extended her arms, inviting Trisha and Amber to take her hands. Soon, they'd used their hands to create an unbroken circle.

Grace offered, Clarissa took the side of her fork and cut off a sizable piece of her omelet. She ate it straightaway then washed the bite down with pomegranate juice. The chewy vegetables, egg and cheese blended well with the tart pomegranate juice. Soon, Clarissa was leaning forward cutting another piece of the omelet. She was still chewing the omelet when she pulled her black laptop to the left of her plate. "Oh my goodness," she said, shocked and relieved to see dozens of regional and national women's sex slave trafficking support organizations and shelters. "Tragic that there's a need for these organizations and shelters," she grimaced. She spent the next half hour searching for the names, street addresses and telephone numbers of nearby shelters that offered housing for women in danger.

At the end of her search, she fell back against the kitchen chair. The kitchen was empty, not a trace of Trisha or Amber, which sent Clarissa's gaze darting from the back door to the dining room until she glanced down at the table and saw that, except for her plate, glass and silverware, all of the dishes, including the skillet that she'd cooked the omelet in, had been washed.

Scrubbing and rinsing her plate, fork and glass was a quick work. It was also gratifying due to the fact that it had been years since anyone had cleaned up for her. Her dishes drying in the drainer at the side of the sink, Clarissa returned to the table. She leaned over the table and looked at the notepad that she'd written the names, addresses, telephone numbers and email addresses for shelters on. "Trisha and Amber," she called out, figuring the girls were in one of the guest bedrooms.

"Yes?" Trisha hollered from the top of the living room stairs.

"How are Amber and you doing with the search for where Wanda and Jackie might be?"

"Jackie's from Atlanta," Trisha called down the steps. "So, she probably headed this way. I say we search the Androssa and cheap hotels around here to see if she shows up. She probably can't afford to stay at the Androssa. But, she might have gone back there to see if that woman would help her. Either way, she'll have to stop somewhere and rest. She couldn't walk all the way from North Georgia here without stopping."

"Is that what you did?" Clarissa asked, walking to the bottom of the stairs and looking up at Trisha. "Did you stay overnight at cheap hotels?"

"No," Trisha told her. "I stayed in a sewer once like I told you. Another night, I holed up in a cave. I was too scared to risk going to a hotel." She paused. "But, I could see Jackie staying at a hotel." Shaking her head, she added, "She's not the type to stay outdoors overnight. She'd be way too scared of wild animals to even try to do that by herself."

"And where do you think Wanda headed?" Clarissa asked.

"Wanda's from Philadelphia. I think she headed north or with Jackie."

"Okay." Clarissa turned away from the stairwell. "I say we start scouring the Atlanta area, looking for Jackie. Then, tomorrow we head north in search of Wanda. But, first let me make a few phone calls." After a pause, she asked, "Did you find any specific places where you think Jackie and Wanda might be? I don't want to just drive. Don't think that's the smartest way to go about finding them."

"We listed six hotels that we think Jackie might have stopped at. We can stop at those hotels and ask the managers if they've seen her."

"This may be a silly question, but do you have a picture of Jackie and Wanda?" Clarissa asked.

"No," Trisha said. "But," she added, suddenly smiling. "I drew a picture of them while Amber searched the Internet."

"You're an artist?" When Clarissa climbed the stairs, she was holding her cell phone.

"The pictures look a lot like Jackie and Wanda," Amber said, suddenly too shaken to manage a smile. "Trisha is a good artist."

"I hope you don't mind." Trisha looked up from where she sat in front of the guest bedroom dresser next to Amber. "I used pencils and paper I found in this top drawer."

"You did the right thing," Clarissa said, glancing at Amber who she thought had become far too quiet. "Those sketches are damn good. They may be a blessing. While I make a few phone calls, will you both please map out the closest route from the Atlanta hotels that you listed, so we go from hotel to hotel without having to drive in circles?"

"Sure," Trisha said. "Who are you calling?"

"Women's shelters." Spotting Amber's taut brow and half open mouth, she said, "Women's shelters know who to tell what. They have lots of experience doing what it takes to keep women and children safe."

Trisha looked at Clarissa. "Thanks."

"Yes," Amber nodded. She kept her focus on the laptop that was placed atop the long dresser that Trisha and she sat in front of. "Thanks."

"I want to do this," Clarissa told them. "I want to find Jackie and Wanda. Just one more thing," she said, raising a finger.

"What?" Trisha asked.

"We're going to be back out on the road in half an hour. The sooner that we find Jackie and Wanda, the better. Every hour matters. At this point, it's like an hour is an entire week. We gotta get moving. And, this time you don't have to sit scrunched down. Just find a way to keep your heads below window level."

Seconds later, Clarissa exited the guest bedroom, entered her own spacious bedroom and sat on the edge of her bed dialing the first woman's shelter. As the conversation neared its end, she asked the woman on the other line, "Can I email you a picture of the two missing girls?"

"Sure. Pictures will definitely help."

"Thank you," Clarissa said. "Please keep a radar out for these girls."

"Absolutely."

The last number that Clarissa dialed was her sister, April. An unnerving feeling, a growing knot in the pit of her stomach, prompted her to create a conversation trail with her sister. "Hey, April," Clarissa began as soon as April picked up the telephone.

"Clarissa," April sang across the line. "How are things with you?"

"Life is good," Clarissa answered, a stab of guilt picking at her conscience. "How about you?"

"Still busy as ever at work and at home. Doesn't matter where you work, people want so much from you."

"That's a fact," Clarissa said.

"Glad that you called," April said. "I need to talk with someone who's not going to ask me to do something." She sighed. "I tell you, I have been working day and night these last few weeks. After I finish this project that I'm working on, I'm going to spend a romantic weekend with my man." Her next words were preceded by a snap of her fingers. "Topic switch, but gotta share. Here's an idea," she said. "For your next novel, write a hot, juicy romance."

"You're ready for that romantic weekend," Clarissa chuckled.

"You bet. Girl, I saw this steamy movie last night. Romance is always the best storyline." She laughed. "And, speaking of romance, maybe it's in the cards for you to meet an awesome man. Who knows," she shrugged. "After you meet that guy, I bet the romance novel starts flowing."

Clarissa laughed. "Where am I going to meet this amazing   man?"

"He could appear out of nowhere. Maybe he'll show up while you're at that North Georgia cabin. Or, maybe you meet this guy while you're traveling. You love hitting the road. No telling who you might meet while you're driving around. He could be at the next restaurant you dine at."

"I guess you could be right," Clarissa said. After a pause, she went to say, "April—"

"—What?" April asked after another pause bridged their conversation.

"Nothing," Clarissa said. "You've got me going with this mysterious man coming out of nowhere and all this talk about romance."

"I knew it," April laughed. "You're thinking about some handsome man."

"We'll see what happens while I'm out and about," Clarissa said, glancing toward the guest bedroom that Amber and Trisha sat in.

They talked for another ten minutes, bouncing from the topic of romantic relationships to travel, work and family. Twice, Clarissa nearly confessed to April that she was sheltering Trisha and Amber. Fear of her sister's reaction prevented her. As much as she trusted her sister, she was not willing to jeopardize Trisha's and

Amber's safety. April would promise not to tell a soul about the girls. That much Clarissa knew. Trouble was that she also knew how inept April was at keeping a secret.

This time, she wouldn't blame April if she called their father, troubling him with worry, then went on to call the police, demanding that they bring Trisha and Amber into the station to corroborate their stories. Howbeit, and as easy as it was for Clarissa to understand April's anticipated behavior, she didn't have the courage to risk the girls' safety. Her commitment to saving Trisha and Amber was creating a strengthening bond between the girls and her.

After she ended her conversation with April, she sat on the edge of her bed examining the slight tremors that had started to settle into her hands.

Half an hour later, Clarissa and the girls were heading out of the townhouse door. Clarissa hurried onto Interstate Seventy-Five North. She didn't know why, but she couldn't shake the feeling that Jackie was fifty or so miles north of Atlanta. So, despite Trisha's pleas, that's the direction that she drove in.

Ninety minutes into their drive, on a road off Interstate Seventy-Five just outside of Chattanooga, Tennessee, Amber sat up, pressed her face against the back right passenger window and screamed, "Is that Jackie? Who's that girl walking down that small hill?"

Trisha slid across the seat and leaned over Amber's shoulder.

"Over there," Amber pointed and screamed. She started rocking back and forth, bouncing on the seat.

"Okay. Okay," Clarissa responded, flipping on her blinkers and pulling over to the side of the interstate.

"Hello!" Amber hollered out of the window that she'd rolled down.

"Hello!" Trisha screamed next.

"Jackie!" Amber screamed, tears rolling down her face. "Jackie! Jackie!"

The woman continued to walk.

"Jackie!" Trisha and Amber screamed.

The woman didn't turn.

The Camry's tires rolled over rocks at the side of the interstate as Clarissa pulled onto the shoulder then brought the car to a stop. "Ma'am," Clarissa leaned across the front seat and called out. When the woman didn't turn, Clarissa glanced into the rearview mirror and told Trisha and Amber, "Let me get out. Stay here."

Chapter Nine

Clarissa stepped outside onto the interstate's shoulder and rounded the front of the Camry, leaving Amber and Trisha sitting in the back of the car with their faces pressed against the window. While the girls stared through the window, Clarissa ran down the small incline. "Ma'am," she tried.

The woman wore a yellow and blue t-shirt with 'Memorial Hospital' printed in blue across the top right, front and a pair of black cotton walking shorts. She didn't look up until Clarissa came within a few feet of her.

That's when Clarissa saw the leashed brown and white pit bull. The dog's tail went straight back, signaling that it was ready to fight.

"Excuse me," Clarissa said, stepping away from the woman and her dog.

The woman pulled out a set of ear plugs. "Who are you?" she asked. Her brow was raised. She was on as high alert as her dog.

"I apologize," Clarissa said, raising her hand and shifting between eyeballing the woman and staring at the dog. "I don't mean any harm. I'm looking for a runaway girl named Jackie."

"My name's not Jackie," the woman said, shaking her head with distaste.

"I apologize," Clarissa repeated. "Have you seen a girl out here while you've been out?"

After a pause, the woman said, "No. I haven't seen anyone since I've been out walking. I walk this way at least three times a week. Well, at least since I injured my leg while running quarter mile intervals back at the high school track."

Clarissa recalled her high school track and field days. "I know about running intervals," she said, hoping to build trust with the woman. "I ran track and cross-country in high school."

"Then, you know how challenging intervals are," the woman smiled, pulling back on her dog's leash.

"Thank you for answering my question about the girl. She's in a lot of trouble." Clarissa searched the woman's face.

"What's the girl look like?"

"She's five feet, seven inches tall and weighs about one hundred and forty pounds," Clarissa said. "She's bi-racial and about your complexion."

"Oh," the woman said. She peered up the hill at the interstate. "I haven't seen anyone out here."

"Okay." Clarissa started walking back up the hill.

Near the top of the hill, she stopped. turned and asked, "Have you seen a white van lately?"

"A white van?" The woman squinted. Her narrowed gaze let Clarissa know that she was open to helping.

"The van is dirty," Clarissa said. "It has a Texas license plate."

The woman looked across the interstate and shook her head.

"Thank you," Clarissa smiled. She turned and resumed her walk back to her car.

"Wait," the woman called out. She jogged up the hill behind Clarissa. "I might have seen a van with Texas plates." She squinted, as if trying to locate a specific memory. "But, I can't remember if the van was white."

Clarissa turned and faced the woman. When she glanced toward the Camry, she didn't see Amber or Trisha. Guessing that they were hunched down in the back seat, she kept talking with the woman, except she talked fast. "Were you here when you saw the van? Did you see the van today?"

"No. Not today. Maybe two days ago."

"Did you see who was driving the van?" Clarissa asked. She glanced over her shoulder at the Camry. She started to back step when she still saw no sign of Amber or Trisha.

"I'd never seen them before, and don't remember exactly what they look like. But, it was two men. I'm pretty sure of that. They had beards, kind of like a goatee."

"Thanks. Were you here when you saw the van?"

"No. I was over by the Chenault Mall. It's a small strip mall about five miles from here. I was coming out of a gift shop when I saw the van. The guys were in the van driving out of the mall."

"The men were alone?" Clarissa asked.

"Yes," the woman nodded. "They were alone. As far as I could tell, they were alone."

"And you only saw the van once?"

"Yes. I only saw it once." The woman paused. Then, she raised her free hand, the one not holding the dog's leash. "Come to think of it, it was a white van. Yes," she nodded. "It was a white van. I'm certain of it." She paused. "But, now I'm not sure about the tags."

"Thank you," Clarissa said. She resumed her walk to her car. Her pace had picked up, causing her walk to border a trot. She darted her gaze, searching the car's interior for Trisha and Amber. Her mouth opened when she walked around the front of the car and saw what appeared to be an empty back seat. As rapidly as she was breathing, she waited until she slid across the driver seat, closed and locked the door before she called out, "Trisha? Amber?"

"We're here," Trisha answered. "We were on the floor hiding under the green blanket."

"Good thinking," Clarissa said, turning on the car's engine and pulling away from the shoulder back onto the interstate. A blue Hyundai Accent, followed closely by a silver Chrysler Voyager, sped down the interstate in the left lane. Except for a red pickup truck approaching in the distance, Clarissa had the right lane to herself.

They weren't a quarter mile down the interstate when Clarissa told them, "She wasn't Jackie. But, you probably figured that out."

In an unexpected retreat from reticence, Amber added, "We saw her dog and knew she couldn't be Jackie."

"Did she know anything? Had she seen anything?" Trisha asked, sitting up in the back seat.

"She saw a white van at a Chenault Mall which is where we're headed," Clarissa said, looking for the nearest place in the interstate to make a u-turn.

It was a smooth five miles to the Chenault Mall, yet long enough for Amber and Trisha to drink a bottle of lukewarm water. Once at the mall, Clarissa parked next to a curb, then she hurried inside a beauty shop and bought four wigs, four long silk, print scarves, two pair of nylon pants and four Panama roll hats. "Here. Put these on," she told Trisha and Amber after she returned to the car and tossed the white "Style By Design" shopping bag into the back seat.

Trisha and Amber leaned across the back seat while they tore the price tags off two of the wigs, scarves and hats then jammed the fashion accessories atop their heads. The scarves, one blue and green, the other orange and yellow, they wrapped loosely around their necks.

"Who are these other two wigs, hats, scarves, shirts and pants for?" Trisha asked, the bag laying across her lap.

"Wanda and Jackie," Clarissa told her. "Who knows? We just might need the getup to get them to safety when we find them."

"Yes," Trisha sighed. She pulled the wig further down on her head.

The instant that Clarissa looked into the rearview mirror, her shoulders buckled and for the first time since Trisha and she had crossed paths, she laughed hard, absent care. She laughed so hard, when she spoke, her voice broke up. "You-you-look-so-much-old-older," she said, wiping tears from the corners of her eyes. "Look at each other," she laughed. "Look at yourselves."

Trisha's shoulders quaked almost immediately when she looked at Amber, really looked at her, taking in Amber's sad eyes, the brown hat pressed snug on her head and the green and blue scarf wrapped gingerly about her neck. "You look like you could be my aunt."

The corners of Amber's mouth twitched. She covered her face with her hands. Then, just as quickly, she lowered her hands and looked at Trisha again. Her twitching mouth turned up, then opened into a burst of laughter.

"Do you look like yourselves to each other?" Clarissa asked, chuckling. Her hands rolled forward then backward on the steering wheel.

"We don't look nothing like we normally do," Trisha said. "If I saw Amber from across the street, I wouldn't know it was her."

"Same here," Amber agreed.

"Okay. Good," Clarissa said. "Keep the scarves over the bottom half of your faces. Walk naturally. We're going to check every store at this strip mall. Figure it's best that you both join me this time because you know what Jackie and Wanda look like. All I have are the sketches that you made, Trisha. I've never seen them in person. You both have."

Akin to young children and as if their safety was deposited in what Clarissa did, Trisha and Amber stayed close to Clarissa as they exited the Camry then entered the mall. They pulled the hats down over their foreheads and walked with their heads bowed until Clarissa whispered, "Hold your heads up. We have to look natural, so we don't draw unwanted attention."

Adhering to Clarissa with a tinge of anger, having grown weary with being told what to do since the men had deceived them into slavery, Trisha and Amber raised their heads and moved closer to Clarissa as they passed a sneaker store. Clarissa led them in and out of the sneaker shop quickly, Brooks, Altra Rivera, Nike, Adidas and Puma running shoes lining the store's glass exit doors. There wasn't a store that they didn't enter and speak with a cashier in, showing the cashiers the sketches of Jackie and Wanda.

Several times, Clarissa stepped aside and bid Amber, who chose not to speak despite Clarissa's encouragement, to share details about Jackie's and Wanda's physical build, hair and voice. Trisha, on the other hand, peered above her hat's front edge and told the cashiers, "Jackie is tall, about five foot, seven inches. She's half black and half white, and she walks flat footed. Wanda is Puerto Rican and has long reddish brown hair. She has big, brown eyes. She's medium height, about five foot, five inches."

"Haven't seen them," more than a dozen cashiers answered. "They haven't been in here, at least not while I was here."

At the next to last store that they visited, a casual-wear shop feet away from the mall's rear exit, twenty-five foot show fountain and a Dairy Queen, Clarissa tried a different approach with the cashier. Instead of simply asking the red-haired cashier if she'd seen Jackie and Wanda, Clarissa pressed the teenager, encouraging her to, "Please look at the sketches again.

Look closely. Take your time. Are you sure you haven't seen these two girls in the last three to four days? You might have seen them outside the mall. You might have seen them in the mall, at a restaurant, another store or right here in this clothes store where you work."

"You know, I think I did see someone who fit that description," the cashier said, leaning over the store's long glass counter and pointing at the sketch of Jackie. She moved closer to the sketch that Clarissa had placed on the counter and said, "She was in here the day before yesterday."

Clarissa stepped back. "Do you know which direction she headed in?"

"She headed across the street toward that gas station," the clerk said, pointing to a Sunoco station across the street from the mall.

"Thank you," Clarissa smiled nervously at the cashier. She thought about leaving her name and cell phone number, but she didn't want to risk giving her contact details out to the wrong person. So, instead of giving the cashier a way to reach her should Jackie turn up at the store again, she just looked at the cashier and repeated, "Thank You."

Seconds later, Trisha, Amber and Clarissa were gone. Their last chance spot to check was a pizza restaurant, a joint that proved less productive than any other spot at the mall.

"Where to now?" Trisha asked when they climbed back inside the Camry.

"Across the street to the gas station. Look. It's right there," Clarissa said pointing to the Sunoco across the street from the Dairy Queen.

She pulled the Camry up to the front of the gas station convenience store. "I've got the sketches," she told Amber and Trisha. "Keep the get-up on and stay in the car. Should be quick," she said, opening her door.

"Yeah. I saw that girl," the gas station attendant told Clarissa after she pushed the sketches beneath the bullet proof partition. To her right were rows of scratch off lottery tickets.

"She came in here day before yesterday," he said. "She looked sad, lost," the man said. "I asked her if she was okay and she didn't say anything. She came in here, used the bathroom and left."

"How about the other girl?" Clarissa tried, pointing to Wanda's sketch.

"No," the man shook his head. "Haven't seen her."

"Did you see which direction the girl you did see headed in?"

"Yeah. I did." He walked to the end of the counter and looked out the gas station entrance doors. "She headed toward that sidewalk." He shrugged. "Guessing that she was going to the apartments up that hill to the left. The apartments are about a mile from here."

"Thank you," Clarissa told him. She hurried out of the gas station, got back in her car and drove across the street to the sidewalk area that the man had pointed to. Next, she took a left turn and headed up a steep hill. She didn't stop until she reached a small apartment complex. There were only six apartment buildings in the complex. "Wonder if Jackie knows this area," Clarissa said.

"It looks nice," Amber offered, sitting up enough to see out the back passenger window.

"It does look like a nice area," Trisha agreed, sitting up and looking out of the other passenger window. Her chin rested on the window's interior edge.

Clarissa parked in front of the apartment complex's management office. It was a small red brick building with a red steel door and one two-pane window.

"Come inside with me," she told Amber and Trisha. "We're the only ones out here right now and there's only that small window. I don't feel comfortable leaving you out here by yourselves."

Clarissa entered the office first. Walking to the far, left corner, she approached the office's only desk. "Hello."

"Hello," the apartment manager, a tall, slender woman sporting a salt and pepper afro, replied. She glanced around Clarissa's left then her right side at Trisha and Amber. "How may I help you?"

Clarissa pushed the sketch of Jackie across the top of the chipped, double-pedestal wood desk. "Have you seen this girl?"

The apartment manager scanned the sketch. "No," she told Clarissa. "She hasn't been by here."

"Okay," Clarissa said. Like a tulip pushing up from the earth, an idea came to her after she turned to leave. Returning her attention to the woman, she asked, "Have you seen anyone who looks like this girl anywhere you've been over the last three to four days?" She shook Jackie's sketch in front of the woman. "Anywhere? The grocery store? By a hotel? A Walmart? A Target? Anywhere?"

"No," the apartment manager assured Clarissa. "I haven't seen her." She shook her head while she stared at the sketch of Jackie.

"Okay," Clarissa nodded in defeat. "Thank you." Turning toward the door, she extended her hands and pushed the door -- hard.

A tepid breeze went across her face.

"I'll let you know if I see her," the manager stood and promised, cocking her head and watching Clarissa, Trisha and Amber as they exited the office.

"Thank you," Clarissa said, not bothering to leave her contact information.

Four hours later and miles of road ahead of her, Clarissa sighed and said, "Let's go back to my townhouse. I've been driving for hours." She squeezed her hand into a fist. Frustration at how arduous and unforgiving it was searching for someone who'd been kidnapped nearly overcame her. As much as she hated to admit it, the thought that she'd never find Jackie and Wanda was starting to gnaw at her. When she texted Mark and Lois an hour ago, they told her that they hadn't seen anyone around the cabins, a response that had pushed Clarissa deeper toward defeat.

Tightening her grip on the steering wheel, Clarissa turned away from her inner thoughts and told Amber and Trisha, "The lady at the Androssa Hotel doesn't even work at the hotel anymore. And, nobody who was there was any help. On top of that, we must have stopped by twelve other hotels, not to mention half a dozen convenience stores and corner restaurants and nothing turned up at any of them." Closing her eyes, she swallowed her longing, her outright desire, to howl in bitter disappointment, in outright exhaustion. "When we get back to my townhouse, I'll check with the women's shelters to see if they've seen or heard anything." She sighed. "Tomorrow, we head north in search of Wanda." After a pause, she continued, "Oh, and I contacted a detective friend of mine. He's spreading the word about Jackie and Wanda to people in law enforcement who've proven themselves to be trustworthy. They're looking for them too."

Desperate to happen upon Wanda and Jackie yet visited with the weighty fear that they wouldn't, Trisha and Amber sunk down further on the seat. Amber's eyes flooded with tears. Nearly overcome with emotion, her nose had started to run. Next to her, Trisha took in short, shallow breaths.

Chapter Ten

Dew covered the grass like a silk blanket the following morning as Clarissa got down on her knees at her bedside and prayed, begged to find Jackie and Wanda. She prayed "Dear Lords" and "Please Gods" with her fingers locked together while she rocked back and forth on her knees. "God, please keep Jackie and Wanda safe. Please, God. Please help me to find them today." Yet, her pleas seemed to fall like rain, pelting a barren land, earth devoid of seed.

Hope escaped her when she stood, distanced itself from her as if she had a plague. Instead of feeling renewed, she felt an ugly heaviness, an unwanted promise that no matter what she, Amber or Trisha did today, they would be met with failure. It was a debilitating emotion, hard to push through.

Were it not for routine, Clarissa might not have departed her home. Instead, she might have climbed back into bed, curled up on her side and tried to revisit sleep. Yet, routine called for her and she thanked the Creator and pushed her shoulders back. "*Find your resolve*," she coached herself.

That's when she walked to her nightstand, retrieved her cell phone and started dialing women's shelters again. She'd done the same thing less than seven hours ago. Yet, here she was, dialing those familiar phone numbers again.

"Is this the lady who called here late last night?" the woman who answered the phone at the North Georgia women's shelter asked.

"Yes," Clarissa said, embarrassment adding color to her face. "Have you heard anything since last night?"

The unexpected happened, even if only to keep Clarissa on her toes. Raising her voice slightly, the woman said, "Oddly enough, we have--"

"--Oh, my goodness," Clarissa screamed. She immediately covered her mouth, not wanting to alarm Amber or Trisha.

"Early this morning, we received a report of one of the girl's being spotted in Ohio--"

"--That has to be Wanda," Clarissa said. "She's from Philadelphia."

"Is there someone in the Cincinnati, Ohio area you know who could look for her? That's where she was spotted around four o'clock this morning. I was just about to call you. She was spotted outside a grocery store. The store was closed. She might have just been walking by, looking for a place to rest."

"I could call my sister," Clarissa suggested. "But, no," she quickly added, changing her mind, "She'd only worry and get too many people involved. We can't risk that," she said, shaking her head. "I can't do anything to risk those girls getting caught up in that dangerous web again."

"We have a call to the women's shelters in Cincinnati. They're on the lookout. And, they know what to do. But, they haven't seen her. We learned her whereabouts -- if it's her -- through a tip."

"Okay," Clarissa nodded.

"But, if you're serious about finding her, you better get to Cincinnati now. The women who work at the shelters don't drive around looking for people. They have so much urgent work to do on site. If you want to keep this close to your chest and not spread the word about Wanda and Jackie too broadly, risking their pursuers capturing them, you'll have to do that hard work of searching for them on the ground yourself."

"I'm on it," Clarissa said. "Calling the airlines now."

"Smart."

With that, the woman dropped the line.

The next time that Clarissa spoke "Okay" into her cell phone, she was talking with a representative at Higher Airlines. "I know I can beat that price. But, I don't have time to price search. Get me three roundtrip tickets to Cincinnati."

During the silent interlude, the airline representative keyed the three tickets into her electronic system. While she did, Clarissa stood next to her nightstand rubbing her forehead. "Oh, and the tickets are for minors, girls under eighteen. They don't have a driver license or passport. Is that okay?"

"Sure," the representative answered. "Minors can still fly our airlines without official identification. That may change in the future, but they can fly now without a passport or driver license. However, TSA may require a copy of their birth certificate to get through security. You might want to check with TSA at the Cincinnati airport." After a pause, the representative asked, "Can I help you with anything else?"

"No," Clarissa answered, already starting her search for identification requirements at the Cincinnati airport.

"If there's nothing else, you're all set," the representative said, shaking Clarissa away from worry. "The first confirmation number is--"

Clarissa punched the speaker button on her cell phone, sending the representative's voice booming thru her bedroom, then she raced to the other side of her bedroom for her backpack which she jammed a pair of jeans, a t-shirt, underwear and socks inside.

"Please just email me the information for all three tickets," she said just as the representative started to read the last confirmation number.

The next sound that Clarissa heard was a dial tone. She didn't bother to check her emails before she walked to her bedroom door and, raising her voice, called down the hall, "Our plans have changed."

Trisha and Amber sat silently on the edge of the queen sized bed in a guest bedroom. They were fully dressed. They sat close to each other, silently finding comfort in one another's body heat. The last experience that either wanted was the experience of feeling alone.

"Yes," Trisha responded.

"We're going to step up our efforts to find Wanda and Jackie. This time, we're going to fly to Cincinnati, Ohio and see if we come across Wanda. I'll rent a car at the airport and we'll drive until we spot Wanda," she'd told them. "A woman's shelter received a report that Wanda had been spotted in the area. We have to go."

And so, as it had been since they'd met, Trisha and Amber followed Clarissa, went along with her ideas.

If only Clarissa's ideas would pan out.

Notwithstanding the mad dash to pack and race out of the townhouse, the actual direct flight to Cincinnati was smooth. Reflecting back, Clarissa thought that the toughest part of the sudden travel was the drive from her townhouse to the Atlanta international airport. As was customary, once she had driven onto Highway Four Hundred, she had hit a wall of traffic, trucks, SUVs, compacts and full-size cars moving nearly bumper-to-bumper down the highway. She'd spent the next forty minutes zipping in and out of different lanes, none of the lanes moving faster than forty miles an hour.

Now aboard the airplane and pressing her head into the seat headrest, she closed her eyes and sighed. Relief transformed into appreciation as she recalled how she had been able to get Trisha and Amber through airport security absent a driver license or passport. When she opened her eyes, she still held onto appreciation that Amber and Trisha were minors, allowing them to fly absent official identification.

She stared at a magazine picture of a De Palm Island beach cedar cabana. Although she had little interest in the cabana or the other contents of the in-flight magazine, she found herself flipping through the magazine's pages. "Have either of you been to Cincinnati before?" she asked, tiring of sitting next to Amber and Trisha in silence. She received Amber's previous day's reticence, a mood that appeared to have worked like contagion on Trisha, with distaste.

When neither girl spoke, she turned, and her shirt collar pushing against her neck, she eyeballed them. Frustration turned to anger and she reminded herself that they really didn't know her, that they were all three actually strangers forced together by emergency.

For Clarissa, the remainder of the flight proved long and slow like old molasses dripping out of a hole at the bottom of a damaged plastic bottle. She didn't speak another word to the girls. Next to her, Trisha and Amber had settled into a one-on-one discourse, shutting Clarissa out.

When they landed in Cincinnati, they grabbed their bags out of the overhead bin and headed for the rental car area. Amber and Trisha followed Clarissa. While she shadowed Clarissa, Amber couldn't stop staring at a girl with long, wavy reddish brown hair. Before Amber knew it, she was walking toward the girl.

Had they been walking within a crowd, it would have escaped Clarissa that the girls were no longer trailing her. But, she quickly picked up a change in the distance, the growing faintness of the footsteps that had once been loud behind her. Her mouth formed an "O" shape when she turned and saw Amber and Trisha walking toward the girl.

Rather than to chase after them, Clarissa stood still, akin to one of the nearby boutique mannequins. In one hand she held her book bag, absent her familiar Glock. In her other hand, she carried the black and orange travel bag that she'd shoved two pair of jeans, two blouses, two pairs of socks, two toothbrushes and two pairs of underwear for Amber and Trisha in. They were her clothes, as were the jeans, t-shirts, socks and underwear that Amber and Trisha wore. But, Clarissa had come to see the garments as belonging to the girls.

"Wanda?" Amber whispered after she got within arm's reach of the girl with the reddish brown hair. "Wanda? Wanda?"

Trisha held her breath. She twisted the wig on her head, straightening and tightening it in place.

"Wanda?" Trisha tried. "Wanda?" she asked, walking so close to the girl that she spotted two pin-head sized pimples on the side of the girl's face.

The girl turned. She looked right at Amber then at Trisha. She didn't speak.

Taking in the girl's wide, green almond shaped eyes, Amber and Trisha stepped back. Their mouths turned down.

"Apologies," Trisha told the girl. "We thought you were someone else."

That scene played out several times. It was becoming a routine, a sign that Trisha and Amber were starting to think that every girl with long, wavy reddish brown hair could be Wanda.

Clarissa clutched her book bag strap while she looked across the airport terminal hallway at Trisha, Amber and the fourth woman with reddish brown hair that the girls had stopped.

As Clarissa watched the woman roll her eyes and pull out of Amber's grasp, she approached Trisha and Amber and, leaning toward Amber's shoulder, she told them, "Let's search the bathrooms. Amber, you said if you'd gotten close to an airport in Georgia that you would have flown home. Who knows?" Clarissa shrugged. "Maybe Wanda has a similar plan. Maybe she saved enough money to fly home."

With a series of head nods and apologies, Trisha and Amber moved away from the woman and followed Clarissa further down the terminal. They hadn't walked a quarter mile when they looked up and saw a quartet of women, two dressed in jeans, one in a pant suit and the other wearing a calf length sleeveless pastel, spring dress, standing in line outside the first bathroom that they came to.

The line moved slowly, but it moved. Scent of a heavy duty cinnamon air freshener whisked up Clarissa's nose when she entered the bathroom. "Please wait here," she told Trisha and Amber, turning and looking over the crest of her shoulder. "I have to pee."

As soon as she came out of the stall, her book bag now hoisted over her back and the black and orange travel bag still in her hand, she spotted Trisha and Amber. They stood with their hips pressed against the long row of sinks and mirrors. They stared so hard at the women who entered the bathroom that several of the women turned away from looking at themselves in the mirrors, combing their fingers through their hair and wiping glare from their foreheads with Kleenex, and feigned interest in the stall doors.

"She's not in here," Clarissa said after she washed and dried her hands. "I didn't see anyone who looks like her go in and out of any of these stalls. Let's go."

Trisha and Amber followed her, but Clarissa had a growing sense that something about them had changed. There was this lingering unwillingness to comply. She feared letting them out of her sight, certain that they would bolt.

"We have to stay together. We have to do this together," Clarissa told them as they prepared to enter the fifth and last bathroom. Her hands were partly closed, shaped into loose fists. She shook them and said, "We must."

The only response that Trisha and Amber afforded her was to glance at each other then quickly shift their attention to the bathroom door. A pungent odor akin to the smell of dried urine hung in the air in this bathroom. Seeking to shield herself from the funk, Amber pulled up on her shirt collar and covered her nose.

Walking to the last stall, Clarissa placed her hand flat against the door and pushed the door open. She did that to every stall door.

The bathroom proved to be empty, after which Amber groaned, "I knew this wouldn't work. Where are those women from the shelter you keep talking about?" she begged, holding out then shaking her hands.

Clarissa took in a long, slow breath. Then, she let it out again. "Let's go get the rental car and head for the train station."

It surprised Clarissa when the girls moved at a faster pace as they exited the bathroom and hurried out of the terminal. They almost ran across the airport parking lot to the row of rental car booths. Clarissa opened her stride and shadowed them.

"Right here," Clarissa said when they reached the Enterprise booth. She handed the rental car agent her driver's license then stepped back and waited.

When the agent exited the booth again, he held a set of car keys and a touch sensitive tablet. Clarissa followed him as they circled a silver Ford Focus, inspecting the car's exterior for dents and scratches.

"Everything's fine," Clarissa told the rental car agent as they finished circling the car. She signed the rental agreement, grabbed the keys and climbed inside the car.

Trisha and Amber slid across the back seat. They waited until the agent returned to the booth before they pulled down on their wigs.

"Which way to the train station?" Clarissa asked the rental car agent after she put the car in drive and inched the Ford Focus to the front of the booth.

The agent stepped outside the small booth, leaned toward the Focus' driver side door and, pointing toward the exit, said, "Hang a right as soon as you leave this parking lot. Drive about a mile to the Interstate Seventy-Five North ramp. Get off at exit One-D. Turn right onto Gest Street. Then, you'll take a slight right onto Winchell Avenue. Finally, hang a left onto Ezzard Charles Drive. You'll see the train station from there. You can't miss it," he told her. "The train station is about fourteen miles from here."

"Thank you," Clarissa said, punching the accelerator and moving to the parking lot exit. She flipped on the right blinker then sped down the street.

Twenty minutes later, a smile pinched at the corners of her mouth. There it was, the Cincinnati Union Terminal. Water burst upward out of the fountain that decorated the front of the massive terminal, its' main facade an impressive half circle that could be seen from as far away as the street.

Clarissa parked the Focus at the front, right of the terminal. Before she could turn and look toward the backseat, Amber and Trisha were standing outside the car.

"There are mainly Amtrak trains in here," Clarissa said while she walked in step with Amber and Trisha.

Amber pulled the front of her wig further down on her forehead.

"We should be okay," Clarissa told her. "We're a good way from Georgia. You don't have to hide your face."

They walked in and out of crowds at the train station, searching for Wanda and Jackie, mostly Wanda.

"Have you seen this girl?" Clarissa asked dozens of train station employees. She showed so many people Wanda's picture that the paper the image was sketched on started to tear around the edges.

"No," came the familiar, fatiguing response. "I haven't seen her."

Two hours later and her feet aching, Clarissa grimaced. The ache, coupled with the unfruitful search for Wanda, sent a tremor into her chin. She blinked fast and fought back tears. "Let's go get something to eat," she told Amber and Trisha. "What do you want? A salad, a burger, pizza?"

"Pizza sounds good," Trisha said. Suddenly, she stepped back. It surprised her to see Clarissa's chin tremor.

Clarissa's show of emotion pressed Trisha to retreat again into quietness, made her feel uncomfortable. Yet, it gained another result as well. It chipped away at the distrust that she'd placed in Clarissa after Amber assured her that they -- because of the horrors that they'd experienced -- could not afford to invest trust in another human being.

"How about there?" Amber asked, pointing at a New York Style cheese pizza sit-down restaurant.

"Lead the way," Clarissa told her, weary with decision making.

They each ordered a slice of cheese pizza and a medium lemonade. Heat pushed off the pizza when their waiter brought the food to their table, a small blue square table close to the cash register, away from the terminal walkway.

"Take my hand," Clarissa smiled at Trisha. She extended her other hand toward Amber.

The girls gave each other a telling glance before they placed their hands inside Clarissa's.

"Dear Lord," Clarissa began, her head bowed and her eyes closed, "Thank you for this nourishment. Please bless our journey so that we find Wanda and Jackie on this very day. Amen."

"Amen," Amber echoed. She reached for her napkin, shook it open and placed it on her lap.

Trisha sipped her lemonade before she said, "Amen."

After she folded her pizza slice in half and took a bite, Clarissa suggested, "Why don't we stay at a hotel tonight. I'm exhausted. We'll head back out in the morning. I say we drive as far as Columbus, Ohio or maybe even to the southern part of Indiana tomorrow. Then, we catch a flight and head back to my townhouse." She paused, no longer chewing the pizza, and smiling into, "It would be great to have Wanda and Jackie with us on that flight."

"Absolutely," Trisha and Amber agreed.

This time and while becoming increasingly aware of how Clarissa was responsible for every speck of food that she'd eaten over the last two days, silence felt awkward to Amber, so she worked at small talk. "This train station is big. It's got a historic look to it."

"Yes," Clarissa said, taking another bite of the pizza. "This train terminal was built in the 1920s. Part of the terminal's history is on display right in this place," she said, turning and looking over her shoulder. "About ten minutes ago, we walked past the visitor center where a lot of that history is on display."

"Oh. That was over by the Omnimax Theater?" Trisha asked, wiping her mouth with a napkin.

While they engaged in chit chat, they kept looking toward the walk area outside the restaurant, eyeballing travelers as they sauntered by, hoping to see Wanda, spot her in the crowds. With one last bite of pizza and another drink of lemonade, Clarissa wiped her mouth and asked, "Ready to go? We can stay at a hotel near the train station or airport."

They ended up staying at the Accordian Hotel, a thirty-two-floor hotel close to the train station and the Ohio River. The hotel had an Olympic sized swimming pool, fitness center, on-site restaurant and a convenience store. Clarissa booked a one night stay. After she let the girls in the room, she stepped out into the hallway and called her sister, April, mainly to say "Hello" and to keep a telephone trail going.

"If you want to go to the pool, I'll buy you a swimsuit," Clarissa offered after she re-entered the room, a writing desk and two queen sized beds, the top edge of the blankets rolled down, greeting them. She hoped that Amber and Trisha would accept her offer so that she could be alone. She had begun to tire of looking at their dour expressions.

But, she was not to be satisfied as she heard Trisha answer, "That's okay."

"Well, I say we settle in for the night," Clarissa responded. She turned her back to the girls, who had sat on the bed closest to the enormous casement windows, and shut her eyes tight.

"We just want to find Wanda and Jackie," Amber sighed. She stood and looked out the windows at the street below, watching cars and buses pass.

"We have to find Jackie and Wanda," Trisha said, her voice gaining strength and volume. Soon, she was screaming, "We have to find Jackie and Wanda." Her face was contorted, making her look like a stranger to Clarissa and Amber. It scared Trisha to hear herself scream, strength to repress her growing fears giving way. She fell back on the bed and buried her face inside her hands.

"Finding them is taking too long," Amber argued. She balled her fists and slammed them against her chest. "No one is helping us. No one at those shelters is helping us."

Clarissa stood with her back to the girls for several minutes, taking deep breaths, working to steel her nerves. When she turned, she went to the television, picked up the remote and tapped the power button. That single motion introduced a technological-makeshift caretaker into each of their lives. They curled on the beds and watched one movie after another, until they drifted into sleep.

While they slept, night cloaked the city in a thick darkness. The moon, a few honking horns and noisy katydids and crickets served as meek clues that the city was yet alive.

The clock at the side of Clarissa's bed showed two eighteen. After stirring in bed and turning from her left to her right side, she moved away from sleep. Light from the television made it hard for her to keep her eyes closed.

She stared at the television screen and hoped that Trisha and Amber wouldn't waken, as she sat and pushed to the bed's edge. An image called to her. It was a black and white drawing, obvious work of a professional artist. She couldn't take her gaze off the television.

Across the room from her, Trisha had stirred herself awake in the other bed. The covers were pushed beneath her chin.

Suddenly never minding the girls, Clarissa stood, walked to the television and turned the volume up. The sketch of a girl, akin to the drawing that Trisha had made of Jackie, hung like an albatross at the upper right side of the television screen.

Tossing back the covers, Trisha crawled to the front of the bed. It only took her seconds to make out the image. "No," she screamed. Her voice went out like a siren, overtaking noise that the katydids and crickets made outside.

Trisha's shouting voice worked like magic. Amber bolted up like a jack-in-the-box. She stared at Trisha, then she looked at Clarissa. The last place that she looked was at the television. Her gaze settled on the image with painful curiosity. As she'd done when she first happened upon the other girls at the small Indianapolis office, the first place that the sex traffickers had gathered them, Amber took a long time exploring the girl's face. She took note of the girl's wide eyes, her short cropped bangs, her long forehead.

Leaning forward in a single slow motion, she stared at the girl's face. An entire moment passed before she sunk down in the bed, not in search of warmth or comfort but to hide from the crushing fear at the center of her chest. Instead of screaming, she buried her head in her hands and rocked back and forth.

Clarissa stepped forward. As if taking up where Amber had left off, she gawked at the television.

The newscaster's voice was slow, even. "The girl who was reported missing two years ago has been found," he said. "Tragically, the girl named Jackie Davis was found drowned in the Chattahoochee River ten miles outside of Atlanta."

Trisha pulled her knees toward her chest and moaned like she'd been struck in the stomach by a wrecking ball.

Amber stared at the window's edge. Tears went like hot water down her face.

Clarissa wiped away tears. Then, she snatched her cell phone off the nightstand.

Chapter Eleven

Two days later, the trip to Ohio surfacing only pain, Clarissa was driving down Roswell Pike in Sandy Springs, Georgia. Red, pink and yellow daisies waved like miniature flags beneath the mild summer breezes that passed through the area like refreshing breaths from heaven. Cars, trucks and a few motorcycles went down the two lane road like all drivers traveling through Sandy Springs were in a dreadful hurry. Way in the distance stood the tall queen and king buildings, their top floors saluting the firmament. Blue skies and rising temperatures let on that the time of day was somewhere between noon and late lunch.

Despite the rushing traffic, there was a tranquility in the day that powered Clarissa with appreciation. It was Saturday and yet it felt like a lazy, Sunday afternoon. Even now, Clarissa dared to hope. She just petitioned her beliefs to protect her from outright exhaustion should her hope return with only emptiness, not even a sense of defeat. Just-flat-out-nothing.

In the back seat, Trisha and Amber sat linked in the same sorrow, the very same fear. Their bodies leaned together, the crown of their shoulders touching. The wigs that they wore made them look old, as if they had experienced more than they should have. As the Camry sped up the road, a soft song played on the radio. Trisha and Amber scarcely remembered hearing the song before, but the melody and the woman's voice came to them with a striking familiarity. Sarah McKin was the artist. Her gentle voice went like melancholy through the song that kept repeating the same refrain that had the song's title in it, "reaching the end of the road with my best friend."

Becoming aware of the impact that the song might be having on the girls, Clarissa punched the third button on the radio dial, interrupting the song and bringing Selena Morgan's "Losing You Is Hard" into the car. No sooner did the song reach the second stanza did Clarissa glance in the mirror, absorb Trisha's and Amber's drooping shoulders, and punch the fourth button on the radio dial, bringing Legacy's "If Not For You" across the airwaves.

For all the sweetness in the song, the girls didn't move, not until Trisha leaned all the way across the seat, passed Amber, and pointing a finger which she shook, called out, "There's Wanda. There's Wanda."

"Wanda," Amber rolled down the window and screamed. "Wanda," she hollered at the top of her lungs.

Following the sound of Amber's voice, Clarissa turned on her right blinker and pulled the Camry to the side of the road. "Wanda?" she called out.

The woman, her reddish brown hair pulled back in a ponytail, stopped walking. Less than one hundred yards away was a truck stop. The name "Flatgrill Diner" flashed across a neon sign that hung at the front of the truck stop. The woman looked toward the Camry, but only for a second. Then, she started to run. She sprinted toward the diner.

Clarissa put the Camry in drive, punched the accelerator and raced inside the truck stop parking lot. The lot was filled with semis, eighteen-wheelers, cars and passenger vans, most which looked older than seven years. Across from the truck stop was a wooded area.

Trisha and Amber leaped out of the car. They ran with abandon.

"Stop," Clarissa yelled after them.

Ignoring Clarissa's plea, Trisha and Amber ran faster. Their legs ate up more of the parking lot pavement; their arms swung wildly as they ran.

Fearful that one of the guy's hunting the girls could be hiding behind the diner's back corner, Clarissa shifted into an all out sprint and caught up to Trisha and Amber. She grabbed them by their shirt collars, forcing them to slow to a stop. The next words that she spoke were breathy. "We have to be smart," she snapped. "We don't know who's here." Shaking her head, she looked at the girls and said, "It might not be safe."

"Well, what are we going to do?" Trisha stammered. "Stand here and lose someone else?"

"We can't keep pulling back," Amber shouted, stomping the ground. She leaned forward, and with clenched fists, she dared Clarissa to try to pacify her. "It's time to make a move, I don't care how risky the move is. Playing it safe is only going to get another one of us killed."

"I'm calling a friend," Clarissa responded hurriedly, pressing a speed dial number on her cell phone. She couldn't bare to lose another girl, not after seeing the news piece on Jackie. Even if she became hyper vigilant, she'd rather take extra precautions now than sit back and respond to whatever happened.

Amber and Trisha eyeballed each other. Then, they looked toward the sky and rolled their eyes.

"Gregory, it's Clarissa," she said as soon as her friend answered.

"What's up?" Gregory said. "You good? I hear stress in your voice."

"No. I'm not good, and I don't have time to talk," Clarissa admitted. "Do you know where the Flatgrill Diner is on Roswell Pike in Sandy Springs?"

"Yeah.".

"Can you call Paul and Carter and get here now?"

"Should be able to," Gregory said, his words coming out slow.

"What's wrong?" Clarissa asked. Her brows rose.

"Joann's been having chest and stomach pains yesterday and today," he revealed, rubbing his forehead. "Could be a bad reaction to the fish that we ate a few days ago. Don't know," he shrugged. "She's stable. She's at home. Plus, she's tough," he smiled. "You know how strong Joann is."

"I do," Clarissa nodded. "Hate to ask, but If you can make it, please come now," she begged. "It's urgent."

"All right," Gregory said. "Let me tell Joann. Then, I'm on it," he told her. "Are you safe?"

"At this very second, I am." She paused. "Hey, Gregory?"

"Yes?"

"I'm with two girls who escaped a sex slave trafficking ring."

"Is this what you called about a few days ago? Are these the girls you asked us to be on the lookout for?"

"Yes."

"Hang up. Lay low. You know how to handle yourself. Let me call Paul and Carter," Gregory said. "Dudes in those sex slave trafficking rings are like a hard mob."

Two minutes later, Clarissa's phone rang. It was Gregory. "We're on the way. I'm about fifteen minutes from where you are. Paul should be there in half an hour. Carter should be there in less than twenty, twenty-five minutes," he told her. "Lay low until we get there. Be smart. Be sharp."

"I will." With that, Clarissa hung up the call.

"Help is on the way," she told Trisha and Amber. A deep frown line formed at the center of her forehead, "You two might not believe this," she told them, "But, I've already done and continue to do a lot for you. I'm doing a lot to save you and Wanda." She swallowed hard. "For now, let's get back in the car." Shaking her head, she added, "We just don't know who's out here."

"No," Trisha argued. "I'm not going back to the car. We have to get to Wanda. We have to save her."

"Yes," Amber agreed, planting her feet firmly on the ground, as if preparing to fight. "We have to protect Wanda. We can't leave without her."

"No way are we leaving without her," Clarissa said. "But, we have to be safe. It's not going to do us any good if we get Wanda only to have a group of men grab all of us."

Trisha and Amber searched Clarissa's face, her set brow, her fixed gaze. Then, turning and looking at each other, they hung their heads in defeat.

"I can't pretend to understand what you both are feeling and thinking right now," Clarissa said. "But, I have to protect both of you and I have to rescue Wanda too."

Their shoulders slouched and their feet heavy like large cement slabs that they dragged across the ground, the girls turned and followed Clarissa back to the Camry. As soon as they reached the car, Clarissa opened the back door and said, "I apologize that we have to do this again. But, I need you to get in the back seat and stay out of sight. I'm going over to Wanda. Thanks to you, I know what she looks like. I really believe it's her. She was scared hearing somebody call her name. That's why she took off running. The good news is that she saw me with you. She should know that it's okay to speak with me. I've got to get us all to a safe place."

Clarissa hadn't taken three steps away from the Camry when she turned back, opened the back door and asked Trisha and Amber, "Why do you think Wanda would be out here by a truck stop? Isn't this the last place that she'd want to be?"

"What if they caught her and are making her work truck stops again?" Amber cried.

"No," Trisha moaned, falling back against the seat and pulling the green blanket up over her shoulders.

"I'm going into the Flatgrill Diner to bring Wanda out. This diner is about ten miles from my townhouse. But, I don't get this far down Roswell Pike often. I only know this area a little bit," she said. "If anyone approaches the car or knocks on the door or window, don't answer. Stay beneath the blanket until I return."

A man startled Clarissa when she turned. He stood less than five yards from her, staring at the Camry. He had dirty blond hair and wore a pair of worn jeans and a blue and white t-shirt. Gray hair salting the front of his hair caused Clarissa to think that he was in his mid-fifties.

Clarissa didn't budge even as she and the man locked gazes. They continued to stare at each other while the man walked passed her, one awkward uneven step after another. And, that's when Clarissa's gaze shifted down to the man's knees and his ankles. The man walked with a hard limp, mainly favoring his left side.

No longer sensing him as a threat, Clarissa turned and watched the man until she saw him climb inside a blue Subaru and drive out of the parking lot.

The man gone and falling into a sense of safety simply because she was in the parking lot alone, Clarissa left Trisha and Amber to bid for themselves and ran toward the diner, two elderly couples sitting on the only wood bench out front. On each side of the bench was a white, waist high ceramic urn. The pointy ends of a handful of plastic flowers were pushed down in a piece of green floral foam at the bottom of each urn.

The closer that Clarissa got to the bench, the more she made out Wanda, her troubled face, her reddish brown hair pulled back into a long ponytail. She watched Wanda move with a brisk stride as Wanda made her way across the back of the parking lot, bordering the woods. At first, Clarissa wondered why Wanda hadn't run inside the diner, seeking temporary safety if only because, once there, she wouldn't be alone. Then, Clarissa turned, shadowing Wanda with her stare, and remembered that there was a mall nearby, busy with shoppers until nine o'clock at night. The mall was three blocks behind the diner. Her memory serving her better, Clarissa knew that Wanda could cut through the woods to take a shortcut to the mall, but the longer that Wanda walked without entering the woods, the more Clarissa convinced herself that Wanda had her wits about her.

Just as Clarissa went to call for Wanda, beckon her close by gifting her with the mere sound of her own name, a tall fortyish man wearing a black knit button-down shirt and a pair of tan khaki pants raced after Wanda, barking, "Come here."

Clarissa stood back, as if she'd now only come to the diner to be a witness. She watched Wanda hurry along the top edge of the parking lot, head toward a sidewalk that led to the mall.

"Wanda," the man snarled. "Wanda," he called out, lunging forward.

The two couples sitting on the bench turned and looked in Wanda's and the man's direction. But, Wanda and the man only held their interest for a second. Soon the couples were turned back around, facing each other, talking and laughing until the gums of their dentures showed.

Across the parking lot, the end of Wanda's shirt collar blew up when the man brushed her shoulder. Clarissa felt a sour taste fill her mouth while she watched the man's face turn up into an ugly frown, revealing his anger at his inability to take firm hold of Wanda.

Fear that she'd lose sight of Wanda shook Clarissa away from observing the scene as if she were a member of an audience. Thinking fast, she ran away from the diner toward a man carrying a plastic bag filled with bottles of water.

"Excuse me," Clarissa called to the man.

The man opened the cab door to his eighteen-wheeler and, tossing the plastic bag across the seat, he started his climb inside the truck.

Clarissa searched the man's brown eyes, the black in his beard. "I need your help," she told him.

The man, his frame a medium five foot seven inches, kept one foot on the truck step. His other foot was still on the ground. "Yes?" He leaned to the side and looked behind Clarissa.

"I'm alone," Clarissa told him. "I know you don't know me. But, this is urgent. This is serious." She talked fast. "I'm pleading for a young girl. Please," she begged, clasping her hands together and peering up at him. "I'm begging you to do me a favor. It's for the girl over there by the woods, the girl with the ponytail."

Following Clarissa's pointing finger, he turned and looked toward the edge of the woods. "She's your daughter?" He shrugged. "Why don't you just go get her?"

"Her life is in danger," Clarissa stammered. "Please," she begged, turning and looking over her shoulder toward Wanda. "That man by her is very dangerous. He could kill her. I'm not asking a lot. Will you just approach her and ask her to go with you for a hookup? Then, lead her back to the Flatgrill. After you get her back to the truck stop, I'll go to the area where you're sent and knock on the door. That's your signal to bring her out." She looked at the man and waited.

"What the hell is going on?"

Clarissa rubbed her hand back and forth across her forehead. "She was kidnapped. These men force women into prostitution. Please," she begged. "This is the only way to get to her, to free her."

"Damn," the guy muttered.

"Please," Clarissa asked, her eyes wide, her clasped hands shaking.

"Okay," the man nodded. "But, if you're a cop, I'm taking you to court." He held up his cell phone, letting

Clarissa know that he'd been recording their conversation.

"I'm not a cop," Clarissa assured him. "But, three male friends of mine with special forces training are on their way here. They should be here soon. Backup is on the way," she said. "No one's going to get hurt."

"You don't know that for sure," he told her. "But, okay," he said, pulling up on his belt.

That's when Clarissa saw the gun hanging off the side of his belt.

Pulling his shirt hem over the gun and stepping out of the truck, then closing and locking the door, he told her, "Let's go."

"Remember. Just go over to the girl with the ponytail and tell her that you want a hookup and get her back to the Flatgrill," Clarissa whispered from where she walked two steps behind the man.

"Got it."

"I'm going to follow you from a distance," Clarissa said. While she followed him, she texted Gregory, asking where he was, urging him to hurry.

"Hey," the truck driver called out, taking long strides toward Wanda. "You owe me a job. You're not going to stiff me. We're going back to the Flatgrill. You owe me."

"You better listen to him," Clarissa chimed. She stepped around the truck driver and ran to Wanda's side.

Wanda jerked away from her.

Clarissa grasped her forearm and mouthed, "Amber and Trisha are with me. Don't say a word."

Wanda looked from Clarissa to the truck driver.

"Hey," the guy in the khaki pants bellowed. "She's with me." Turning and looking at the truck driver, he said, "You have to go through me to get to her, Buddy."

Clarissa didn't take her eyes off of Wanda. "Go with me back to the Flatgrill," she mouthed.

Wanda looked toward the sidewalk, grass and dandelion springing up through the cracks, then she turned and looked at the Flatgrill. Another look at Clarissa and she pivoted, abandoning her earlier goal, and started walking toward the diner.

"Smart girl," the guy in the khakis said. "You know what to do," he grinned. "You'll like her," he smiled at the truck driver, revealing a front row of chipped teeth.

"How much?" the truck driver asked the guy in the khaki pants as soon as they reached the edge of the Flatgrill.

The guy laughed. "So, this is how it works. You go inside and pay the guy at the cash register enough money to cover how much time you want to spend with her." He grinned at Wanda. "That guy at the cash register owns the diner and the truck stop." Tapping the truck driver's shoulder, he added, "When you get to the cash register, keep your voice down."

"Okay," the truck driver said, looking at Wanda.

"One hour," Clarissa whispered as she followed the truck driver and Wanda.

"And, you," the guy in the khakis said just as Clarissa neared his side. "You must be one cool lady. This your birthday gift to your man?" he nodded, grinning and tilting his head toward the truck driver.

Clarissa paused, then quickly answered, "Of course."

"How about that? There are some decent chicks in this world," the guy in the khakis chuckled. He stood several feet from the diner door, choosing to stay outside.

The two elderly couples, oblivious to what had just occurred within feet of them, relished in a joke and let out a roar of laughter as Clarissa entered the diner. The door squeaked to a close behind her.

A long breakfast counter was the first item that Clarissa saw when she entered the diner. Three pastry trays topped with donuts, fruit pies and brownies filled the glass dessert cabinet. On the other side of the pastry trays was the diner's only cash register. The truck driver approached the cash register and lowered his voice to a whisper. "How much for an hour with her?" he asked, glancing over his shoulder at Wanda who now stood at his side.

"Two hundred dollars," the guy at the cash register said, his voice smooth, easy.

The truck driver dug to the bottom of his jeans and pulled out his wallet. He handed the guy at the cash register four fifty-dollar bills.

"There's a room all the way at the back. Entrance to the sleeping quarters is right there, less than ten yards to the right. It's connected to the diner," the guy at the cash register said, tilting his head toward the end of the diner. "You'll see the room back there. It's the last door on the right," he added, handing the truck driver a small key.

The truck driver glanced over his shoulder at Wanda and she followed him into the sleeping quarters. They entered the small room at the back where there was nothing more than a twin bed with a soiled mattress covered with a thin sheet and an old floral comforter. At the side of the bed was a cheap, splintered nightstand on which was a light green lamp.

While the truck driver and Wanda entered the back room, Clarissa ordered a bottle of water and a cherry pastry, as a decoy, a way to cover her tracks. She took a slow bite of the cherry pastry, then she stood and peered out of the diner's glass door. When she didn't see the guy in the khakis, she opened the door and searched the parking lot. As soon as she spotted the guy over by a row of fuel tanks, pumping gas into a green Plymouth Voyager, she hurried out of the diner and walked back to the Camry.

She tossed the bottled water and pastry across her passenger seat as soon as she unlocked the Camry. "We're going around back," she told Trisha and Amber, not daring to look over her shoulder, fearing that she was being watched. "There's a truck driver who's helping us free Wanda. He took her to a room at the back of the truck stop."

"Hurry," Amber shouted, sitting up and pulling on the back of the seat. "It's a setup."

"There are other guys nearby," Trisha said. "This is how they work. There are always two to three more of them nearby in case a man decides not to pay or tries to run off with a girl."

"Shit," Clarissa cursed. She snatched her cell phone out of the car cup holder and texted Gregory. A moment later, she said, "My friend is less than five minutes away. I'm going to the back of this truck stop. We have to go now. There's a guy in khakis we have to avoid. He's olive complexioned with jet black, oily hair. He can't see us from where's he's pumping gas in a green van. Thankfully, he doesn't know what my car looks like." She released a breath. "This is not going to turn out bad. It can't." She shifted the Camry out of "park" and drove to the back of the truck stop.

"Stay here," she said after she parked the Camry between four cars at the back of the truck stop. "More than ever, you need to stay here," she repeated, grabbing her Glock out of the glove compartment. Then, she exited the car, popped the trunk and pulled a bag stuffed with a wig, a pair of green nylon pants and a shirt with a hood out of the trunk. After she closed the trunk, she shoved her Glock in her waistband and hurried toward the door.

She knocked on the door three times, each knock louder than the one before. Thump-thump-thump her knuckles rattled against the wood.

No one came.

Thump-thump-thump, Clarissa tried again, this time leaning her ear close to the door.

No one came.

Clarissa jerked the knob back and forth. She pulled on the knob. Then, balling her hand into a fist, she banged on the door.

This time when she listened, she heard approaching footsteps. She held her breath and placed her finger on her gun's trigger while she watched the knob turn from the other side.

She closed her eyes and sighed when she saw the truck driver's brown eyes. He peered outside, looking at Clarissa then over her shoulder at the cars parked toward the far end of the truck stop. "Hurry. Come in," he said, stepping back and giving Clarissa room to enter.

Clarissa squinted, adjusting her vision to the dark narrow hallway. "Where is she?"

"Follow me." He walked to the room that he'd escorted Wanda inside less than five minutes ago.

They reached the room door and the truck driver said, "You go in first. I want to make sure that no one followed you."

Clarissa shook her head. "No one followed me." She turned the knob slowly. Then, she entered the room. Her face turned down when she saw Wanda sitting on the edge of the bed, her hands folded in her lap, awaiting whatever would follow.

"You can get up," she told Wanda. "Nothing is going to happen to you."

Wanda eyeballed the truck driver, as if awaiting his approval to move.

"Like I told you when we first came back here, I'm not going to touch you," the truck driver told Wanda. "We never were going to have sex. We're going to get you out of here."

It startled him when Wanda didn't smile.

"No one's going to hurt you," Clarissa assured Wanda, reaching for her shoulder.

Wanda pulled away from Clarissa. She looked at the truck driver for permission to move.

"I'm not going to touch you in any sexual way," he repeated. "That's not why I brought you in here." Looking at Clarissa, he added, "This lady is your friend. She's looking out for you. If it wasn't for her, I'd be in my truck headed for Oregon."

"Okay," Wanda nodded, glancing at Clarissa.

"We're going out the back door," Clarissa said. "We have to hurry."

"I paid for an hour," the truck driver told her.

"Yes. But, they're bound to have lookouts," Clarissa said.

"Put this on," Clarissa told Wanda. She pulled the clothes and wig out of the bag that she'd carried from her car.

The truck driver walked to the other side of the room and faced the wall. While he did, Wanda changed clothes. Then, she pulled on the wig. She looked at Clarissa and ran her hand down the front of the clothes and patted the sides of the wig.

Clarissa smiled. "You look fine." Then, she reached out and took hold of the sides of the wig. "All this wig needs is a little straightening."

"We're ready," Clarissa turned and told the truck driver who had busied himself watching a cockroach scamper up the wall.

They hurried to the door. "I'll go first," the truck driver said. He turned the knob. Then, he peered through the small opening. Seeing an empty hallway, he motioned to Clarissa and Wanda to follow him.

They moved like thieves down the dark hallway, their shoulders hunched, glancing over their shoulders toward the diner. The truck driver exited the back door first, checking for strangers before he pushed the door open far enough to allow Clarissa and Wanda to exit.

"Hurry. Hurry," Clarissa said, tapping Wanda's back, nearly pushing her inside the back of the Camry. "Get under the blanket." Wanda hidden, Clarissa closed the passenger door and hurried to the driver door. "Hop in," she told the truck driver. "I'll drive you to your truck, so you're not spotted."

There was no sight of the guy in khakis as Clarissa drove the Camry around the corner. She pulled alongside the trucker's cab door. "Thank you," she told him, patting his hand then pushing two one hundred dollar bills beneath his palm.

With a nod, the truck driver squeezed the money and climbed out of the Camry. Once inside his truck, he pulled on a baseball cap and a pair of sunglasses. After he turned the key in the ignition, the truck's engine sent a deep hum across the lot. He kept the cap's front brim pulled over his eyes as he pressed the accelerator and pulled out of the parking lot.

Behind him, Clarissa turned the Camry in a semi-circle. Just as she got the Camry pointed toward the parking lot exit, two men ran toward her.

One of the men raced to the passenger side of the car. He had a hard, large square face with a raised, protruding forehead. The other man slapped his right hand against the driver side door window. Both men were hefty, standing six feet and weighing more than two hundred pounds. They wore white muscle shirts, advertising that they pumped iron.

"Stay down. Stay under the blanket," Clarissa ordered the girls who continued to hide in the back seat.

The men banged on the car windows with the side of their fists. With their other hand, they jerked on the door handles.

Clarissa laid her foot on the accelerator, sending dirt and gravel flying into the air.

The men clung to the door handles, refusing to let go.

Clarissa drug them through the parking lot. She didn't press the brake until two other men ran right in front of the Camry. That's when Clarissa swerved the Camry to the right, then sharply to the left.

"Stop, thief," one of the men near the front of the Camry shouted. He pointed at the Camry. "That lady kidnapped my daughter's friend." he shouted.

Soon all four of the men were shouting "Stop, thief. Kidnapper."

Diners raced out of the Flatgrill. They ran toward the Camry. Some people got close enough to see inside the car.

"Call the police," an onlooker shouted.

So many people circled the Camry until Clarissa could no longer drive without hitting someone.

"Stay down," she told the girls. "I don't care what happens. I don't care what you hear. Unless I tell you to get up, stay down. Stay out of sight and don't move."

Just then Clarissa turned and saw the man standing next to her window catch a pipe that a guy standing at the front of the car had tossed him.

The man next to the driver side swung the pipe at the window.

Clarissa's gaze darted across the parking lot. She was desperate to find an opening large enough to get the Camry through and speed out of the parking lot.

The man kept swinging the pipe, banging the window, shaking the car, until Clarissa heard the glass start to give way. When she looked down, she saw bits of glass spewed across her lap.

"Don't move," she ordered the girls.

She pressed the accelerator, forcing the onlookers to step away from the front of the Camry. But, she wasn't fast enough.

The man swung the pipe again and the glass broke, leaving a gaping hole in the window. Blood sprinkled out of the man's arm when he reached inside the broken window and started punching Clarissa's face.

Out of the corners of her eyes, Clarissa saw the man next to the Camry's passenger window swing the pipe at the passenger window. That's when Clarissa reached for her glove compartment.

She pulled out her Glock and pointed it at the man who was swinging the pipe. As soon as the man stepped back, she pointed the gun toward the man next to her.

The man lunged for the gun.

A loud pop noise sounded across the parking lot and the man standing next to the driver side window stumbled backward.

When he regained his footing and lunged for her a second time, Clarissa pulled the trigger again, shooting him in the stomach. This time when she looked at the man, she saw blood spotting his shirt.

No longer concerned with the growing crowd, the guy on the passenger side aimed a gun at Clarissa's head.

Chapter Twelve

Clarissa sunk down in the seat, but not before she saw Gregory, his car tires squealing, speed inside the parking lot, trailed by Paul and Carter.

Gregory jammed his foot on the brake, bringing his Dodge Charger to a screeching halt one car over from where Clarissa was parked. He jumped out of the Charger, crouched below the door handle, and hurried toward Clarissa. By the time the guy next to the Camry's passenger window spotted him, it was too late. "Drop it," Gregory ordered the man, pointing a pistol at the side of the guy's head.

Onlookers scattered. Many ran from the parking lot onto the Flatgrill's outside porch, desperate to avoid danger. What they didn't do was stop gawking at the scene unfolding before them.

Clarissa sat in her car gripping the steering wheel and breathing in deep breaths. She saw a green Plymouth Voyager race behind her Camry, then she watched the guy who'd held a gun to her head run toward the Voyager and jump inside.

"Get in," Clarissa heard that guy yell to the man standing at the Camry's passenger side.

"They're in there," the man shouted back to the three other guys in the Voyager. "The girls are in the Camry."

"Let's go," the guy driving the Voyager shouted. "We have to get out of here. Someone's bound to have called the cops by now. Come on."

Fearing the cops, the man turned and climbed inside the Voyager's open side door. Then, two of the other men yanked the side door closed and the Voyager sped out of the parking lot.

Clarissa popped her glove compartment open and pulled out an envelope and pen. On the back of the envelope, she scribbled the Voyager's license plate number.

Gregory tapped the Camry's window "Are you okay?" he asked Clarissa when she turned and faced him.

"As good as can be expected." She placed the envelope in her book bag's front pocket. Then, she zipped the pocket closed.

"I see they broke your window," Gregory said.

"Yes. But, they only put enough of a hole in the window for the guy to get his hand inside the car. I'm okay," she assured him just before she took in another deep breath.

"I've got to get the girls in the back seat to my townhouse," she said, still taking in and releasing deep breaths. Turning and looking into the back seat, she told the girls, "You can sit up."

Trisha, Amber and Wanda slung the heavy, green blanket off of themselves. They sat up slowly, cautiously.

"This is Gregory," Clarissa told them. "He's a friend of mine. The guys who were after you are gone. They drove off in a van. But, I got their license plate number."

"Good move," Gregory told her. He paused. "You know," he began as Paul and Carter joined his side. "We should stay until the cops arrive. Then, we can all head back to your place."

"Yes," Clarissa agreed.

"A woman standing on the porch over there," Paul began, "said that she'd called the police."

"I figured as much," Gregory responded.

"Thanks for coming," Clarissa told Gregory, Paul and Carter.

"You know that we wouldn't leave you hanging," Gregory smiled. Then, he turned and told Paul and Carter, "Thanks, Man."

"Yes," Paul and Carter nodded.

"I saw you over by that diner checking the place out," Gregory told his friends. "Did you see anything?"

"Nah," Paul said.

"Those guys have worked this truck stop before, according to some of the customers standing on the porch," Carter said. "Not sure if they're involved in prostitution. But, that's probably why they tore out of here. They didn't want to be here when the cops pulled up."

For the next several minutes, Gregory and Carter questioned diners who'd remained inside the Flatgrill, seeking details on the men who'd chased down Clarissa and Wanda. Paul stayed with Clarissa and the girls. After Gregory and Carter questioned a dozen diners, they circled the truck stop owner.

"Got a minute?" Gregory asked the truck stop owner, tilting his head toward the dark hallway.

The truck stop owner looked from Gregory to Carter. He stepped back, taking in their six foot frames. Then, his gaze landed on the guns tucked inside their side chest holsters. "Who are you?" he asked, looking at Gregory.

"We're former special forces," Gregory told him, pulling out his wallet and displaying his uniformed services identification card. He glanced at Carter. "Navy special forces."

"Oh," the owner responded, taking another step back, away from the cash register.

"Don't get froggy," Carter advised.

"Nah," the owner said, shaking his head.

"Good," Carter said. "We just want to ask you some questions."

Searching the owner's face, Gregory added, "Cops are on the way. We just want to ask you a few questions. Who knows?" Gregory shrugged, "We might be able to help you out with the cops."

"Let's go in the first room," the owner said, walking from behind the cash register. "Over here," he said, tilting his head to the right.

Gregory and Carter followed him into a small room. It was four doors up from the room that the truck driver had taken Wanda into.

"How long have you owned the Flatgrill?" Gregory asked. Carter stood close to the door while the truck stop owner stood next to the room's twin bed. As it had been with the room down the hall, the only other furniture in the room was a small nightstand atop which was placed a cheap ceramic lamp.

"Seven years," the truck stop owner answered.

"Oh," Gregory said, extending his hand. "My name is Gregory."

The two men shook hands.

Carter leaned forward and extended his hand. "My name's Carter."

Introductions over, Gregory returned to his line of questioning. "So, you've owned the Flatgrill for seven years. Has it always been part of the truck stop?"

"No. The diner's newer. I've owned the rest of the place for nine years."

"Oh, my bad," Gregory said. "I didn't get your name."

"Barry. Barry Smith."

Figuring the name to be false, Gregory continued with, "Is the business just the diner and truckers coming in here to rest?"

"Pretty much," Barry shrugged, glancing from Gregory to Carter. "Yeah," Barry nodded, a second later.

He looked at Gregory and Carter again. Then, he said, "So, the cops are their way?"

"Yes," Carter answered.

"They don't get around here much. Things stay pretty quiet around here," Barry said. He frowned. "I don't like trouble. There wasn't any reason for anyone to call the cops," he barked.

"But, that's what we want to talk with you about," Gregory said, taking a step toward Barry. "There were some guys here trying to hurt one of our friends. Those guys were also trying to hurt a girl who'd been in one of these rooms." Gregory paused. "Do you know anything about those men?"

"Told you that I don't like trouble. I like things to stay quiet," Barry answered.

"We're just trying to figure out who those guys were," Carter said.

"Especially considering that they were trying to do a lot of harm to our friend and a young girl," Gregory chimed.

"I don't know any men," Barry said, shaking his head.

"Okay," Carter nodded. "But, we'll be sure to tell the cops what we saw and heard and let them know that you own this joint. So, I'm sure they'll be talking with you."

The small room fell silent for a moment. Then, the sound of police sirens crept inside the room, pumping alarm in Barry. The noise started as a muffled whistle growing in the distance then exploded into a piercing, merciless wailing.

Chapter Thirteen

"We'll go tell the cops what we know and give them our contact information should we be able to be of further assistance," Gregory patted Barry's shoulder and said. A second later, Carter and he followed Barry out of the room, down the hallway, back into the Flatgrill and outside.

Barry stood behind the cash register watching Gregory and Carter exit the diner. While he watched them walk further away from him, he rubbed his chin, as if searching for an answer.

****

"Ready to go as soon as we talk with the cops?" Gregory asked Clarissa, when Carter and he returned to the Camry.

"Yeah," Clarissa said; she pulled a napkin out of her glove compartment and wiped sweat from her forehead, a sign that she was still shaken from the ordeal.

"We'll follow you back to your place," Gregory told her. "That is," he paused, "unless you want to stay someplace else."

"No. No," Clarissa said. "I'd always planned to go back to my townhouse.

"We can sleep on the floor," Paul laughed.

"Yeah," Gregory added. "We'll hang around for the rest of the day and maybe spend the night after I check in with Joann and make sure she's still pain free. She wasn't in pain when I headed over here."

"Hopefully, the cops will find those guys who attacked you and pick them up," Carter said. "But, we'll hang out at your place today and maybe tonight to make sure everything's okay."

"So good to hear that Joann is doing better and not in pain," Clarissa said. "I was going to ask you how she was doing. And," she added, "about you all staying for the night to make sure those guys won't find us, we'll see how that goes," she added, glancing toward the back seat. "They've been through a lot," she added, looking at the girls.

"You're right," Gregory said. "Maybe we can stay in your basement for a day, just long enough to ensure that you're all safe."

"Thank you," Clarissa smiled.

Moments later, Gregory, Carter and Paul crossed the parking lot, heading in the direction of four cops who'd showed up.

"Wait," Clarissa called after them, her hand waving through the air.

"What?" Gregory turned and asked.

"Make sure that you tell the cops that the guy at the cash register is in on it," Clarissa revealed once she caught up to Gregory, Paul and Carter. "He took two hundred dollars from a truck driver I used to help get one of the girls to a back room so I could rescue her."

"You're talking about the hefty guy at the front register?"

"Yes," Clarissa said, looking from Gregory to Paul to Carter.

"He told us his name is Barry," Paul said.

Carter laughed. "But, we know better than to believe that."

"We'll tell the cops what you said," Paul nodded at Clarissa.

Deal sealed, the guys turned and resumed their walk toward the four cops.

"You can sit up now," Clarissa told the girls. "And one of you can come sit in the front seat. I know those guys. I've known them, especially the one named Gregory, for years."

"Where did you meet them?" Wanda asked, opening the back door gingerly for fear that the pipe hits to the front passenger window may have damaged the rear, passenger door. Before she exited the back seat, she reached out and squeezed Trisha's and Amber's hands. When they wrapped their hands around hers, she leaned back on the seat. "Thanks for coming to get me." She held onto Amber and Trisha for a moment before she leaned forward and climbed out of the car. After she closed the back door, she stepped forward and sat in the passenger seat next to Clarissa.

"After we get on the road, I'll tell you where I met my friends," Clarissa smiled at Wanda. She turned and told Trisha and Amber, "We'll be on the road for about twenty minutes before we pull up to my townhouse."

Gregory, Paul and Carter bumped fists with the cops then crossed the parking lot, leaving the cops to talk with an agitated yet nervous Barry. Cops grilling Barry, Gregory, Paul and Carter headed for their cars.

Clarissa glanced into the rearview mirror one final time, taking in the outline of the people still lingering outside the Flatgrill, as they pulled out of the parking lot. They were five miles down the road before she felt herself breathe again, before she stopped feeling like she was holding her breath. "I met Gregory and his wife, Joann, while I was serving in the Navy," Clarissa told the girls. Flipping on her right blinker, she turned onto a back road. Large, expensive homes and rows of trees lined both sides of the road.

"How long were you in the Navy?" Wanda asked.

"Four years. Gregory was Navy special forces. He did twenty years in the Navy." She laughed. "I was in the regular Navy. We became good friends. Then, about a year after we met, Gregory introduced me to Paul and Carter." She searched Wanda's face. Then, looking into the rearview mirror, she looked at Amber and Trisha. "Gregory, Paul and Carter are married. They were married when I met them. I know their wives. We used to hang out. But, they don't live real close to me. Gregory lives in Duluth, while Paul lives in Covington and Carter lives in midtown Atlanta. We were fortunate to catch them when we did."

"For real," Amber said. "Duluth and Covington aren't around the corner. Neither is midtown."

"Yes," Clarissa said. "The guys were out and about and just happened to be close enough to get here when they did."

"Do they have daughters," Trisha asked, moving toward the back of Clarissa's seat.

Just as Clarissa went to answer, Amber blurted, "Wanda, you look clean. Were you staying somewhere?"

"Most of the time, I washed in gas station bathrooms. This morning, I had a grocery store bathroom to myself and washed up good there."

"Were you ever in Ohio?" Trisha wanted to know.

"No," Wanda answered with a shake of her head.

"We got a tip that someone who looked like you was spotted in Cincinnati, Ohio," Clarissa revealed.

After a pause, Wanda said, "Wasn't me." A second later, she raised her arm above the headrest and said, "But, look." She stared at a long scar that went from her inner left elbow to the top of her palm.

"How'd you get that?" Amber asked, ogling the scar.

"One night, I heard something growling behind me. I thought it was a wild dog. When I ran and jumped a fence, my shirt caught on the fence's top edge and I got cut bad. It was bleeding for the longest. But, I got away before whatever was growling got me."

"Good thing it didn't get infected," Trisha said. She ran a finger along the top of the scar, finding the scar smooth and thick.

"Yeah," Wanda said. "So, Cla-ri-ssa, what about your friends' families," she tried, working to shift the focus.

"Paul has two daughters and a son," Clarissa told them. "Carter has three boys. Gregory and Joann have a son and a daughter. All of their kids are in high school. Well, all except for Paul's son. He's still in elementary school. They got a late start on family building," she smiled. "He's in the fifth grade."

"Did the guys who are after us see your friends' cars?" Trisha asked.

"They may have," Clarissa said. "If I had to place a bet on it, I'd say they did. But, they didn't see their license plates. I'm pretty sure of that. Gregory, Carter and Paul are too smart to let that happen."

"Do other people live close to you?" Wanda wanted to know.

"Yes," Clarissa told her. "I don't live in the middle of nowhere." Searching Wanda's face, she added, "Someone would hear us if we hollered."

Wanda swallowed hard and leaned into the headrest.

"I won't put you in harm." After a pause, she asked, "Wanda, how long have you been on your own, running from those men?"

"A week. I left when Trisha, Amber and Jackie did." Her face went blank. She turned and looked over her shoulder at Trisha and Amber. "Where's Jackie?"

The car became silent.

"Where's Jackie?" Wanda asked, raising her voice. "Where is Jackie? Where is Jackie?" She started to rock on the car seat, demanding an answer. "Where is Jackie, damn it?"

"She didn't make it," Trisha said, turning and looking out the window.

"What do you mean, she didn't make it?" Wanda stammered, looking from Clarissa to Trisha to Amber.

"We don't know what happened to her," Amber said. "We were watching the news after Trisha and Clarissa found me and that's when we heard that a girl's body had been found." Amber bit her thumb nail. "As soon as I saw the picture flashed up on the television screen, I knew it was Jackie."

"But, maybe it was somebody who looked like Jackie," Wanda tried.

"They said her name on television," Amber said, shaking her hands at Wanda.

"It was Jackie," Trisha assured Wanda. "We didn't want it to be her either. We drove miles looking for her and you," she said. "I was starting to think that we might not find you." Pulling in her bottom lip, she said, "I'm so glad we found you. I'm so glad you're okay."

"Is that what you all were doing out here?" Wanda asked.

"Yes," Amber told her. "We've been looking for you for more than a day."

"They refused to go home without you," Clarissa told her. She kept her thoughts about how Amber had become more conversational since Wanda showed up to herself. "They wouldn't even contact their parents until they found you for fear that their parents would contact the authorities, some which might be crooked, and put you in danger."

Wanda sat still, soaking up what she'd just heard before she asked, "Trisha, where did you go after we all split up?"

"I headed straight for the river. That led me to a highway. I stayed close to the highway, but down in a ravine, so no one would see me from the road. I ran in the daytime," she told them. "At night, I hid outside or in garages and basements. It's summer, so I was able to find houses with the basement window open. I crawled in and went to sleep. It was a good way to hide. Even though I was scared someone might come in the basement and find me, it was a lot better than being trapped with those piece of shit guys."

"Yes," Wanda said. "I'm so glad we found each other." She sat back on the seat. Then, she leaned forward again, turning and looking from Clarissa to Amber to Trisha. "Do you think Jackie's parents know what happened to her?" She paused. "Where was Jackie found?"

"A good way from here," Clarissa interjected. "Probably about eighty miles from here."

"She drowned in the Chattahoochee River," Amber said. "I want to know how she got in the river." She shook her head. "She had to have been running from someone."

"You're right," Trisha said. "Someone must have been chasing her."

"Do you think the guys broke up into two teams looking for us?" Wanda asked.

Clarissa steeled her nerves and tightened her grip on the steering wheel.

"Why do you ask that?" Amber wanted to know.

"Because I feel like someone's been following me since the day after we escaped."

"They might know someone in this area," Trisha said, chewing on her bottom lip. "Atlanta is big for sex slave trafficking."

"Yes," Wanda sighed. "It was probably as easy as making a phone call to get another man to start hunting us."

"It's going to be all right," Clarissa said, squeezing Wanda's hand.

"They might be working with a larger network than we initially thought," Amber said.

"You're right," Trisha agreed.

"Yeah," Wanda nodded. "We can't drop our guard for a second." She sighed. "I hate to think of Jackie out on the road all by herself scared, being run off the road until she finally thought she had no choice but to dive into the river."

"Remember how she would talk about her mom and dad and her adopted sister?" Trisha said.

"She loved her family," Wanda moaned.

"She talked about them all the time," Amber added.

"And remember how Jackie talked about how she was going to make it to the Olympics as a swimmer?" Trisha asked.

They stopped talking.

"That's what I don't get," Wanda said. "Jackie said she was an excellent swimmer." She paused. "Jackie said she was one of the best high school swimmers in the country."

"It is odd that she would drown," Amber admitted.

"Somebody had to have attacked her," Trisha cringed. "She probably bumped her head on a rock or something."

"After we get home, I say we get in touch with Jackie's family. We should let them know how much

Jackie talked about them, how much she loved them," Wanda said.

"We have to," Trisha agreed.

"Yes," Amber nodded.

"Do you all want me to take you home tonight or in the morning?" Clarissa asked, her eyes turned down like soft fruit.

"In the morning," Wanda said. "We need to just be with each other a little longer before we part forever, especially after what happened to Jackie. And, hopefully, those guys will be long gone come morning." After a pause, she continued with, "Trisha and I live the farthest. Trisha is from Indianapolis and I'm from Philadelphia."

"That makes perfect sense," Amber said. "I'm from Atlanta. I could catch the bus home if I wanted to."

"No," Clarissa admonished. "I'm going to take all three of you home." She paused. "Trisha and Wanda, I'll get you a plane ticket home. I'll fly with you and make sure that you get home to your parents."

"Thank you," Trisha said, working at a smile.

"Yes. Thank you," Wanda and Amber echoed.

Ten minutes later, they pulled up to Clarissa's townhouse community.

Wanda leaned forward and looked through the car's front windshield at the flowers, trees and townhouses. "Oh, you live in a gated community," she smiled.

"Yeah. I guess you could say that," Clarissa replied. "I grew up in apartments. I prefer a townhouse to a traditional single home."

"Her place is really nice," Trisha told Wanda. "You should sleep good tonight."

"First time in a long time I'll have slept good," Wanda told them.

"What were you doing in Sandy Springs and by a truck stop?" Trisha asked.

"I was trying to get home and trying to stay in heavier populated areas. I know," she shook her head. "The truck stop area wasn't that busy. But, my online research showed Sandy Springs is nice. I didn't want to go near a truck stop, but I had to. I was trying to get to a mall over there. From the mall, I was going to try to get to the airport. I thought I'd be more safe going through Sandy Springs to get to the airport," she told them. "On top of that, I was hoping to find a place to work for a few weeks, so I'd have enough money to afford a plane ticket to fly back home to Philly."

"Me too," Trisha said. "I thought about what I could do to come up with money to get an Uber to get to the airport so I could get back home to Indianapolis. From where I'd be picking the Uber up, I knew it would cost way more than a hundred dollars. On top of that, I knew walking to the airport would be too much on me physically. Plus, I'd be really risking having the guys spot me if I did that."

"Never thought I'd run into any guy involved in sex trafficking. Definitely didn't think I'd run into a guy who knew my name." Wanda shook her head. "Don't even know how that guy knew my name," Wanda said, clenching her teeth. "Damn. It's like they're everywhere." Glancing out the window, she said, "I'll never be able to trust a man again. They all look so damn clean, but," she added, shaking her head, "Some of them are like wild wolves, just looking for a girl to prey on. Filthy cockroaches."

"You don't have to concern yourself with the cost of a plane ticket anymore," Clarissa told them. She pulled to the front of her townhouse. Pressing her garage remote, she waited for the door to lift. Then, she drove the Camry inside and closed the garage door.

She grabbed her Glock out of the glove compartment, got out of the Camry, popped the trunk and removed her backpack. "You all ready?" she turned and asked Wanda, Amber and Trisha.

The girls nodded and followed her inside the townhouse. Seconds later, Gregory, Paul and Carter pulled their cars up to the front of Clarissa's townhouse.

After Clarissa unlocked her townhouse and let the girls inside, she returned to the front porch where the guys stood leaning against the wood railing that encased the porch. "Let's go around back," she told Gregory, Paul and Carter. "You need a key-pass to get thru the main gate, so we have some safety. But, this isn't the time to take chances," she said, locking the townhouse's front door and walking around back. "We need to talk."

Soon after she spoke the words, she had a change of mind. "Tell you what. I'll meet you on the back porch in a minute." Returning to the front of the townhouse and unlocking the front door, she re-entered the living room.

Trisha, Wanda and Amber were flipping through channels on the flat screen television nailed to the center of the living room's longest wall.

"Looking for a certain show?" Clarissa asked.

"No." Amber shook her head. "We're just looking for something that's not too heavy to watch."

"Well," Clarissa said, picking the remote control off the living room console. "If you press this 'Guide' button, you can see what each channel is showing."

"Yeah, I remember that shit," Wanda said. "It's been a minute, but I remember that remote stuff."

Clarissa's brow was tight when she looked at Wanda.

"Don't mean to curse," Wanda told her.

"You sound like a confident, street smart young lady," Clarissa chuckled.

"For sure," Wanda laughed. "How do you think I made it through all this shit." She took the remote from Clarissa and turned to a drama on the BET channel.

"I'll be out back with the guys," Clarissa said. "Came back inside because I didn't feel like I gave you a proper introduction to my home." She looked toward the dining room. "Feel free to make yourselves something to eat or get a drink of water or tea. And, Trisha," Clarissa said, turning toward Trisha who sat at the far left end of the sofa. "Do you mind showing Wanda were the bedrooms and bathrooms are?"

"Sure. I'll show her after we watch enough of this movie to see if it's worth sticking with."

"And remember," Clarissa said, "Don't answer the door. If someone knocks on the door -- I don't care if it's me -- don't make a sound. Come to the back of the house, look for me or one of the guys and let us know that someone is at the door."

"Yes," Amber and Trisha answered in unison.

"Look. We're not kids," Wanda said, one hand flung down on her hip. "We're not stupid. We know what to do."

Desire to cut her eyes at Wanda nearly overpowered Clarissa. To keep from falling prey to the impulse, she turned her back to Wanda. "Just be careful," she said before she entered the kitchen, where she squeezed half a dozen fresh oranges, added in concentrated juice and poured the mixture inside a plastic gallon serving container. After she stirred the juice with a long wooden spoon, she carried the orange juice and four plastic cups onto the back porch. She didn't bother making orange juice for the girls.

"Care for something to drink?" she asked, placing the orange juice on a small round table on the back porch. The table was placed in front of an outdoor swing sofa that Gregory, Carter and Paul sat on.

"Sure," Gregory said, leaning forward and pouring himself a glass of orange juice.

After Carter, Paul and Clarissa had their own glass of orange juice, Gregory stood from the sofa and sat on the wide back porch rail. "So, what are you going to do with the girls? How long are you all going to stay here?"

"We're leaving in the morning, Gregory," Clarissa answered. "But, first, I have to find flights to Philadelphia and Indianapolis."

"Who's from Philly?" Carter asked.

"Wanda is from Philly," Clarissa answered. "Trisha's from Indianapolis. Amber lives right here in Atlanta."

"Really," Paul said, his brows raised. "How did they all get together?"

"You know how those sex trafficking rings operate," Carter said. "Those crime addicted dudes ship girls all over the world." He shook his head. "Amazes me how they get away with that shit. But, if there wasn't a customer, sex trafficking would stop. Like much crime, it's a money racket."

"It's like street prostitution," Paul said. "No customers, no business."

"Yeah," Gregory nodded.

"Want us to help you find flights?" Paul asked.

"That would be good." She stood. "Let me get my laptop."

The girls weren't in the living room when she made her way back inside. She peered out the window onto the porch on her way upstairs to get her laptop out of her home office. The porch was empty.

"Guess the movie didn't turn out to be to your liking," Clarissa smiled when she saw the girls sitting on the bed in the guestroom closest to the stairs.

"Nah," Trisha smiled back. "We were just up here talking about how we all got away and what we want to do with our lives now."

"Good," Clarissa said. "We're going to look for flights to Indianapolis and Philadelphia. I'm just going to grab my laptop."

"Our parents would pay for our flights," Wanda said.

"I know that they would," Clarissa said. "But, do you think they would panic and call the authorities and put your getting home safely at risk?"

"That's what we said," Wanda shared. "Yes. We did say that earlier." She sighed. "And, that's probably what would happen. My mom and dad would freak. I'd probably be all over the news in no time flat." She released a deep breath. "Pictures and all."

"We'll look for flights and run them by you all before I buy tickets. If you change your minds before I come back up here, just let me know. It's up to you," Clarissa told them, glancing at Wanda.

Hurrying across the hall, Clarissa grabbed her laptop and headed back downstairs. The guys were drinking more of the orange juice when she returned to the back porch.

"Let's get to work," Clarissa said, turning her laptop on.

"Here's a deal for less than three hundred dollars from Atlanta to Philly," Carter said, raising his cell phone.

"What airline?" Clarissa asked.

They spent the next half hour hunting for cheap non-stop flights. After they settled on two flights, Gregory stood and told Clarissa, "We'll fly with you. Let us make sure we get all three girls home safely and that you get back here safely."

"I wasn't going to ask. But, I certainly will accept the escort," Clarissa smiled. "Let me just run back upstairs and confirm that the flights work for Wanda and Trisha."

"I seriously doubt that they'll have a problem with the flights," Gregory told her.

"Yeah," Paul said. "And, how do you know that someone will be at their place when you get there?" He paused. "Are you all trying to surprise their families?" After another pause, he added, "As cool as that sounds, it could backfire."

"Yeah," Clarissa sighed. "But, we don't want to alarm their parents. We can't risk their parents reaching out to authorities and the media. It could tip the sex traffickers off to the girls' whereabouts or even to when they might be home."

"Good point," Gregory nodded. "But, once these girls get home, they could be safe, especially if they stay alert. The guys might not try to get them again." After a pause, he said, "I think you should alert their parents. You could even have their parents come to your place to pick the girls up."

"You're right," Clarissa said. "Let me go get the girls. It might be good if we all talk this through."

"No. No," Gregory shook his head and said, changing his mind. "It may be better if you take the girls to their families. The last thing that you'd want is for something to happen on their parents' end and you not find out about it until it's too late, an accident, somebody gets sick. Anything could happen."

"But, you should tell their parents," Carter advised.

"Let me go get the girls," Clarissa said, walking to the back door. She didn't turn around. On her way up the living room stairs, she stopped and peeked through her living room blinds. She saw nothing amiss on the street.

"Hey, you all," she called up the stairs. "Come downstairs and help us decide what we ought to do about getting you all home." Before the girls could say anything, she turned and went back outside.

"Come out back," Clarissa leaned forward on the back porch swing and told the girls when she heard them in the kitchen.

The girls stood on the other side of the back screen door. They peered at Gregory, Paul and Carter. Their unwillingness to be close to strange men kept them inside.

Following the girls' gazes, Clarissa approached the screen door. "They're not going to hurt you," she said. "Like I told you before, I've known these guys for a long time. They've worked in the military and in law enforcement."

"Some of those bastards who held us captive had served in the military and worked as cops," Wanda snapped.

"They're not those types of men," Clarissa said. "I wouldn't let them in my home if they were." Seconds later, when the girls continued to stand on the other side of the screen door, she beckoned them to, "Come on."

Pushing on the screen door, Trisha stepped onto the porch. Wanda followed her.

Amber stayed back. She peered through the screen door, keeping her hand on the lock. Her attention was fastened upon Clarissa and the guys with so much intent, she looked to be inspecting them rather than simply looking at them.

"Come, sit down," Clarissa said, patting the empty spaces on both sides of the sofa. "You all can squeeze in," she laughed. "Goodness. I remember when I was as sleek as you three." She glanced at Amber who continued to stand on the other side of the screen door.

Gregory, Paul and Carter leaned against the back porch railing.

"Wanda, I think we should get you to Philly first," Clarissa said, opening her laptop. "Hopefully, you'll like one of these flights that goes from here to Philly then, from Philly to Indianapolis." She started pulling up the saved flights. "And Amber, I think you should stay here. I can drop you off at your parents' house before Trisha, Wanda and I head for the airport."

"I want to go with you, Wanda and Trisha," Amber said from where she stood on the other side of the screen door. "How would I know if something happened to you? I couldn't live with myself if something happened to you."

"We'll be in touch with Clarissa," Gregory assured Amber. "As a matter of fact and as we agreed, I say that at least two of us travel with you, Clarissa."

"For sure," Clarissa nodded. "For now, we have to secure flights."

"Lean close," Clarissa told Wanda and Trisha. "Wanda, since you'll be the first stop, please let me know what you think about these flights." Clarissa moved the laptop to the edge of her lap, making it easier for Wanda to see the flight details. "Which flight do you think is best?"

"That one," Wanda said, pointing to a flight that was scheduled to depart Atlanta at six-thirty in the morning. "I want to get home as soon as I can tomorrow."

"I understand," Clarissa said. Then, she moved her laptop to the other side of her lap and asked Trisha, "Which flight to Indianapolis looks best to you?"

"Well," Trisha said, taking the laptop from Clarissa. "There's a two hour layover on that first flight. Let me see if I can find something with less of a layover."

"How about that flight?" Paul said, leaning over Clarissa's shoulder. "It leaves less than an hour after Wanda's flight lands."

"That might be too close," Clarissa said. "If we're taking Wanda to her parents' house, we need enough time to get Wanda home and then get back to the airport."

Gregory chewed his lip. "It's a risk," he said. "But, we might have to let Wanda's and Trisha's parents know they're headed home. That way, they can meet us at the airport. It could prove safer," he added.

"You know your parents best," Clarissa said, turning from Wanda to Trisha. "Do you think that we should tell them?"

"It is a big risk with my parents," Wanda said. "My mom can get strung up so damn fast. But, it might work," she said. "We can tell them not to tell anyone we're headed home. We'll stress how important it is that no one know where we are or that we're almost home."

"Yeah. That's what I say we do," Trisha said. "But, we don't tell them until the last minute. My dad's dope, but he can be a hot head. I can see how this could go wrong."

Moments later, their flights were ticketed. Then, Clarissa grabbed her cell phone. That's when she said, "You know what? You all need your own cell phones." Glancing at Gregory, Carter and Paul, she asked, "Are you guys up for heading to the nearest Walmart to get them cell phones?"

"Let's go," Carter agreed.

It was a short drive to Walmart. The guys picked up three disposable flip phones. "Can you believe there're only three people in line ahead of us?" Carter joked when they went to pay for the phones.

"We definitely came at the right time," Paul agreed. "And for once, I didn't buy shit I didn't mean to pick up."

Soon they were back at Clarissa's. After Clarissa let them in, Carter tossed the Walmart bag across the sofa. "Got each of the girls a flip phone," he told Clarissa. "These are just temporary. They're cheap disposable phones."

"How much do I owe you?"

"Nah," Carter told Clarissa, waving his hand. "Forget about it."

"Thanks." She gave the guys a once over. "You guys want to head home to your wives?"

"We're staying here tonight. Remember?" Paul told her.

"That's right," Clarissa smiled. "Just make sure that you call your wives."

"We've been texting them since we got here," Gregory laughed.

"They know what's going on," Paul grinned. "And, you know they won't talk," he quickly added.

"You picked good women," Clarissa smiled. "They are super cool."

Suddenly, and as if something had spooked her, Clarissa stopped talking. Her mouth closed fast, like a slammed door. An awkward silence entered the room.

Clarissa shot Gregory a telling glance. Then, she took in a deep breath, her chest pushing out, filling with air. She looked at Amber, Trisha and Wanda. Her voice was deliberate and even when she said, "Time to call your parents."

Chapter Fourteen

Amber hesitated. Then, she moved forward, her footsteps light and slow. She took the black landline telephone receiver from Clarissa. The receiver dangled in her hand as she ran her tongue across her mouth then coughed. Her nerves yet troubling her, she started pulling on her ear and taking in deep breaths. Her shoulders went up then back each time that she inhaled. She looked at Wanda and Trisha, as if begging them for strength. Then, she took another deep breath, punched her home telephone number on the dial screen and waited.

"Mama," she spoke into the receiver as soon as she heard the line pick up. Her hands started to shake, tremoring as if her hands no longer belonged to her, as if a frightened being had taken them over. "Mama."

"Monique, you better not be playing on the phone."

"It's not Monique, Mama." She bit her lip.

"Who-Who is this?" the voice on the other line asked.

"Mama, it's me," Amber cried. "It's me. It's Amber."

"Wha-Wha-What," her mother began. "Am-ber?"

"Yes. Mama," Amber cried, "It's me."

"Mama?" Amber tried again after her mother failed to respond. Several more seconds of silence and Amber started chewing on her bottom lip again.

Her mother started to talk, yet her voice broke up. Still, Amber heard her ask, "What's your middle name?"

"Marie," Amber smiled, welcoming her mother's street smarts.

"What's your father's name?"

"Brian," Amber wept.

The line went quiet, as if her mother had hung up. Then, Amber heard her mother scream, "Thank you, Jesus." Her voice went up like an alarm had sounded. She kept screaming, barely getting out, "Brian, it's Amber." She talked fast, lobbing questions at Amber. "Where are you? Amber, where are you? What happened to you? Where did you go? Are you okay? Are you safe? Can you talk?"

"Mama, I'm safe. I ran away from the men who kidnapped me. I'm with a cool woman. Her name is Clarissa. She's going to drive me home tomorrow."

"Where are you? We're coming to get you right now."

"No, Mama. You can't come here. And, you can't tell anyone that you heard from me. I'll be home tomorrow."

"No," her mother snapped. "Your father and I are coming there right now and we're calling the cops. You should be home," her mother wept.

"Mama, no," Amber tried. "You can't come here and you can't call the police."

"I'm calling the police as soon as I hang up with you."

"No, Mama, no," Amber begged. "You can't call the cops. Promise me that you won't. It could put me and the two girls who ran away with me in danger."

"I'm calling the cops. Do you hear me," her mother pressed.

"Mama, don't," Amber begged.

Carter grimaced while he leaned against the archway that separated the dining room and the living room, the place where Amber stood talking with her mother.

Gregory glanced at Carter and Paul. Then, he groaned and approached Clarissa. Leaning toward her, he whispered, "This is exactly what we didn't want to happen." He sighed. "You know that her parents are going to demand to come and get her now, and I mean right now. Not five minutes from now, but right now."

Pressing the receiver against her ear, Amber continued, "Mama, there were other girls with me where I was. I was kidnapped. I don't want to talk about it now. I just want to get home."

"We're leaving now to get you. Just give me the address. I'm so happy to hear your voice," her mother wept. "Thank God you're okay." A second later, Amber heard her mother shout, "Thank you, Jesus!"

"Mama, I'm going to make sure that the other girls get home okay. Then, I'm coming home. I can't rest until I know we're all home okay. If it wasn't for them, I never would have made it."

"The only place you're coming is home," her mother told her.

"Where are you?" Amber heard her father, Brian, ask. He took the telephone from her mother. "Where are you? We're coming to get you now."

"Dad, please," Amber tried. She hung her head. "I shouldn't have called you."

"Okay," her father submitted, the boom in his voice lowering to a whisper. "Just tell me you're safe. I miss you so much. We just want to see you."

"I'm safe."

Clarissa reached for the receiver.

But, Amber wouldn't let go of the phone. "The woman who rescued us is right here. She wants to say something to you," Amber told her father.

"Hello," Clarissa said, taking the receiver from Amber. "My name is Clarissa. Apologies for talking fast, but two other girls have to call their parents. Your daughter and my paths crossed while I was vacationing at a cabin outside of Atlanta in the country. Your daughter tried to break into a neighboring cabin. That's when your daughter and I met. Friends of mine helped her and two other girls escape a sex slave trafficking ring."

"What?" Brian hollered.

"I know. It is shocking," Clarissa said. "We're happy to drive Amber home today. But, she wants to fly with us to Indianapolis and Philadelphia to drop off the two teens she was held captive with. They all broke free together."

"We want to see our daughter," Amber's mother said.

"Amber," Clarissa began, turning away from the receiver and facing Amber, "Let's drop you off at home now and then, we'll get the other girls to their families tomorrow."

"No," Amber insisted. "I want to make sure Wanda and Trisha get home safe."

Amber took hold of the receiver again. "Mama, I'll call you every hour until I'm back home. Is that okay? Wanda, Trisha and I have been together for all these months." She shook her head. "I'm not leaving them now. They wouldn't leave me. And besides," she wept. "We already lost Jackie. She ran away with us. But, she didn't make it. She drowned. We heard about it on the news."

"I'm coming with you," Amber's mother asserted.

"Amber, we have to take you home now," Clarissa said.

"No," Amber demanded. "I'm not leaving Wanda and Trisha. I already have to live with the fact that Jackie didn't make it. I'm not dealing with losing Wanda and Trisha too."

"Amber," her mother begged.

"Amber," Clarissa tried. "We'll call you as soon as we get to the airport. Then, Wanda and Trisha can call you as soon as they're with their families. Will that work?"

"No," Amber said, shaking her head.

"Okay," Amber's mother relented. "What time will you be home tomorrow?"

Amber looked at Clarissa, who mouthed, "Tell her that you'll be home at seven o'clock tomorrow, definitely before it turns dark."

"I'll be home at seven o'clock," Amber told her mother. "It has to do with the flights."

"Okay," her mother moaned. "But, if you're a second late, I'm calling the police."

"I won't be late," Amber promised.

Trisha's and Wanda's phone calls to their parents were painful, filled with raw emotion and longing. The only thing that calmed their parents was hearing their daughters say, "Meet me at the airport tomorrow. And, don't tell anyone that you've heard from me. You can't tell anyone anything. As far as you know, I'm still missing."

The next two hours went without incident. Then, Gregory's wife, Joann, called. She was different, not her usual laid-back, confident self. Yet, she worked to absolve Gregory of any anxiety her words could birth. "Don't panic. And I don't have time to answer a lot of questions. Just meet me at the Northbay hospital," she told Gregory.

"What's going on?" Gregory asked, raising his cell phone closer to his mouth. "Why are you going to the hospital? Did the pain return?"

"My chest feels tighter than it felt last night. I can't get it to loosen up," she groaned.

"I'm on my way," Gregory told his wife. Turning to Clarissa, he said, "Gotta get to the hospital. Joann's chest pain is back and worse." He grabbed his keys off Clarissa's coffee table. After a pause, he added. "Paul and Carter will be here with you."

"Hold up, Greg," Paul said. "Let me call my wife and make sure that she's good with me staying the night without you being here. She loves Clarissa, but that doesn't mean she's okay with my staying over a woman's house all night without her or you, especially considering that we met Clarissa through you."

Paul was shaking his head when he hung up his cell phone. "Not going to work," he told Gregory. "My wife's not down with me being here if you aren't here."

"Not even if Carter's here?" Gregory asked.

"Nah," Paul said. "Just like I thought, my wife is cool with Clarissa. What she's not cool with is me staying overnight with four females." Shaking his head, he said, "She's just not feeling it. She's good with me coming back here if something happens. Plus, she said Clarissa has military training and doesn't think we really need to stay the night."

"Damn," Gregory chimed. "Just to be safe, Carter, you better call your wife."

"I'll call," Carter said. He was already shaking his head. "But, I already know how it's going to go."

Carter was right. His wife wasn't comfortable with him staying at Clarissa's alone with four women.

Finally, Clarissa told the guys, "We'll be okay here alone. This is the way that it was going to go from the start, before those guys pulled up on us at the Flatgrill and I called you for help." Looking at them, she said, "Remember?"

"Yeah," Gregory admitted. "But, call if you need anything. Call one of us if you see or hear anything. We'll be on standby."

"Yes," Carter said. "Keisha said that I could come back if things start to go sideways here."

"Same goes for me," Paul said. "Zoe knows how dangerous this situation could get. But, she also knows how sharp you are. She knows about your military training."

"We'll be fine," Clarissa replied, wishing that Gregory, Carter and Paul could stay. "It's all right," she added with hopeful nods.

Later that evening, Clarissa and the girls were alone in the living room. Outside the sun was setting, the sky taking on a reddish orange hue. Clarissa didn't think twice about the descent of night, being alone with the girls or the fact that their parents knew about her until she saw her front doorknob jiggle, until she heard someone push hard against the door.

Chapter Fifteen

Clarissa raised her cell phone just below eye level and opened her home security app. Her brows went up and out, leaving her forehead wide while she stared at the image on her phone screen. The man on the other side of the door wore a crisply ironed beige and red utility company uniform. Rather than to turn away from her phone, Clarissa kept her gaze fixed on the man. She didn't stop watching him until he vacated her porch, climbed back inside a utility van and drove away from her home, in the direction of the townhouse community's exit gate.

Then, Clarissa started punching numbers on her phone. Her fingers raced across the number panel. When she looked up and saw the sum of each girl's attention fastened upon her, she worked at conversation. "Let me call the utility company," she said, trying to calm the girls' nerves. Her free hand was shaking behind her back.

"Hello? My name is Clarissa Maxwell. I live at 555 Main Street in Sandy Springs. Did you send a utility service agent to my home?" While she spoke with the utility company call center representative, she turned her back to the girls and uttered a round of "Yesses" "Uh-huhs" and "Okays" into her phone. When she turned back around, the line dead, she told the girls, "Stay inside until we head out tomorrow."

"I should have went to the mall and got to the airport on my own," Wanda whined. "Now, I'm stuck in this house."

Seeking to remove herself from Wanda's disgruntled mood, Clarissa walked toward the dining room. "Do you all like ice cream?"

"Food won't solve anything," Wanda frowned.

"I've got flavored ice water, if you're interested in that," Clarissa tried.

"Maybe we don't want to be fat," Wanda scowled. "And like I said, food isn't going to solve every damn thing. Besides, we just want to go home."

"We're going to do just that in the morning," Clarissa said, rounding the dining room corner.

"I might already be home tonight if you hadn't stopped me when I was over by the diner heading to the mall."

"Those men would have caught you," Clarissa argued. "Plus, you said you needed more money to cover the cost of a flight."

They stared each other down.

"This wasn't my idea, you know," Clarissa told her. "I was on vacation when I was thrown into this--"

"--Oh, well. Isn't that too bad," Wanda said. "Taken away from your comfortable vacation cabin out in the woods. Good thing you weren't forced into prostitution." She turned her lip up, pinching her mouth tight. "Wonder how you would have held up."

Clarissa stared at Wanda for a long time. She didn't speak until she looked at Amber and Trisha and asked, "Ice cream?"

Trisha and Amber glanced at Wanda who stood with her hands planted against her hips. Then, having a longer history with Clarissa over the past forty-eight hours, Trisha left Wanda and Amber standing in the living room and followed Clarissa inside the kitchen.

"Amber?" Trisha turned back and called.

It took two more attempts, but Amber did eventually leave Wanda standing alone in the living room and followed Trisha into the kitchen. Four bowls were on the kitchen table, three filled with vanilla ice cream.

Trisha and Amber sat behind a bowl. But, not Clarissa. She stood at the edge of the dining for a long moment. Then, she stepped around the corner and walked toward Wanda.

"I know that we don't know each other. I really do think I get that much," she nodded. "But, I'm not an enemy. You have less than a day to look at me." She met Wanda's stare. "Why don't you come in the kitchen and enjoy some ice cream, not to solve anything, just to eat one scoop of ice cream."

Wanda twisted her mouth. She didn't turn away from Clarissa, seeing her as no more than a peer. Then, realizing that time, not chance, was on her side, she followed Clarissa inside the kitchen.

It might have been the chill in the ice cream, each girl lapping spoonsful inside her mouth until the cold creamy dessert melted away. Soon all four of them were relaxed, trusting each other enough not to argue. For a short measure, Clarissa and the girls felt free. They felt safe.

Their voices rose and fell with mirth. Clarissa chortled with the girls, but each time that the girls coiled in guffawing, their faces turned toward the table or stove, their voices choking with laughter, Clarissa glanced at the door.

Darkness worked like a cloak, making it hard for Clarissa to see through the back door's top window. And, yet, she was certain that she saw someone scamper across the porch. "Ssshhh," she told the girls. Pressing a finger against her lips, she whispered, "Not a sound."

Trisha, Wanda and Amber leaned into each other, brushing shoulders. It was what they had done while they were held captive and afraid that they would either be beaten or raped. Seeking an eerie solace in their shared trauma was what had drawn them to each other, that and the way that one of them had always fought back, despite how many vigorous blows each demonstration of courage had brought.

As different as they were, their families and cultures appearing as separate parts of a tapestry, they were kindred spirits. They stood up for what was right and they looked out for themselves and each other. "We have to stick together," Wanda had encouraged while they had been held captive. "We're all we've got right now," she'd told them.

Yet, it had been more than Wanda. Each of the girls, including Jackie, her will having been painstakingly eroded by the men day by day, had offered encouragement throughout the traumas. They were young, their lives cast before them like an ocean. They didn't yet know that their experiences had permanently changed them. They did know that they had each other.

Now they were looking to Clarissa, even Wanda with her insistent defiance. Alone and afraid in the kitchen, it was as if Clarissa had become their unofficial protector. Yet, they could have sworn that they'd seen sparks of fear in Clarissa. They'd noticed her shifting gazes and had picked up a slight quiver in her voice. And, so they moved closer to each other.

Clarissa stood. Then, she tiptoed toward the door. Her back was hunched, curled like a big cat's. "Stay down," she turned and mouthed to the girls.

Clarissa held her breath. Then, she slid up toward the bottom of the back door window just far enough to see that whoever was on the other side of the door was wearing a t-shirt. The stranger had the build of a tall, beefy man. His bulky frame stole the little comfort that Clarissa had.

Closing her eyes, Clarissa sank down toward the kitchen floor and hoped and prayed that the man would leave, simply walk off her porch and leave her home.

Yet, that's not what he did. Instead, he stood outside the door for what felt like twenty minutes to Clarissa yet was only two minutes.

Her legs aching from bending toward the kitchen floor, Clarissa tiptoed toward the girls. "Come on," she whispered. "We're going to put chairs beneath the doorknobs and barricade the windows."

They moved with haste, as silent as a hush. By the time they finished, all of the first floor windows had a large glass object in front of them and each exterior doorknob had a chair propped beneath it.

Finally, Clarissa stepped back, eyeballing her living room window and said, "I don't think that anyone can get in here without making a lot of noise." She nodded several times. "It'll be okay. We'll be okay," she nodded.

"Just one more thing," she said, turning at the living room's edge. This time when she checked her security system, the back porch was empty. Relief that she felt was short lived. For the second time, she retraced her steps, sharing, "Gotta check the kitchen one last time."

All that she saw when she looked through the back door window were leaves swaying beneath the balmy evening winds. So, she let the back window blinds fall over her fingers and close then she returned to the living room. After she activated the townhouse's motion detectors, she followed the girls upstairs.

The night passed slowly. Light from the half moon that rested in the sky penetrated Clarissa's bedroom blinds, landing on the ceramic cardinal figure at the dresser's edge, the top of the nightstand lamp and the bottom fold of the green, yellow and purple comforter.

Clarissa turned from side to side, tossing in bed. She listened to see if she'd picked up the slightest noise, a tree limb brushing the window, a dog barking in the distance, footsteps climbing her stairs. Throughout the night, she'd gotten up no less than seven times to pee and look down the dark living room stairwell. The seventh time, she could have sworn that she saw a light flashing in the living room. That's when she grabbed her gun and, tiptoeing downstairs, checked out the first floor.

Seeing nothing, she climbed the living room stairs again. En route to her bedroom, she checked on the girls. They slept soundly in the guestroom.

Then, she entered her bedroom, locked the door, climbed into bed and pulled the comforter beneath her chin. While she turned in bed and gazed into the dark, she wondered who the man on the back porch really was and she wondered where the guy in the utility uniform got the outfit, especially considering that the utility company had told her that they hadn't sent an agent to her home.

Burdens troubling her, she drifted into sleep for a short two hours before she sat up. Groggy with fatigue and unsettled by a full bladder, she stumbled into her en suite. On her way back inside her bedroom, she stopped. She thought that she'd heard a bump, as if something had landed against the living room stairwell wall. "But, no," she thought to herself. "We boarded the place up too good for anyone or anything to get in here." And yet, she couldn't stop thinking that she'd thought she'd seen a light flashing in the living room earlier in the night.

Rather than to wonder if an intruder was in the house, she hurried to her nightstand and grabbed her cell phone. She sent Gregory a quick text, "How's Joann? Slight change of plans. We're leaving for the Atlanta airport now. Should be out of here in less than an hour. After you all left, a guy stopped by in a utility uniform, but when I checked with the utility company, they said they hadn't sent anyone. And, later yesterday, some strange guy was on the back porch. We boarded up good, so I think we're okay," she texted even as her gaze shifted toward the door.

"We're back home from the hospital. Joann's sleeping. Are you safe?" Gregory texted back ten minutes later.

"I think so."

"Be careful. Text me as soon as you land."

Clarissa's phone was still in her hand when she stumbled into her bathroom and layered her toothbrush with toothpaste. Placing her phone on the counter, she brushed her teeth, carefully listening for the slightest noise. Afterward, she lathered her hands with soap and washed her face bare-handed, brushed her hair and, returning to her bedroom, hurried into a pair of jeans and a t-shirt. Then, grabbing her jacket, she rushed into the guestroom. She was quick, reminiscent of the Navy company commanders who'd barked orders at her while she'd been in boot camp.

"Hurry. Hurry," she told the girls. "Get up. Get washed up and get dressed. Our plans have changed. We're leaving for the airport now."

Thirty minutes later, Clarissa and the girls made their way down the stairs, each girl carrying a small bag that held her meager lifelong belongings. "Wait here," Clarissa warned, extending her arm across the front door, keeping the girls behind her. She hurried inside the kitchen and peered out of the back door window and the kitchen windows. Then, returning to the living room, she peered out of the sides of the blinds.

"Let me just check one last thing," she said, reaching for the remote and turning on the living room television. After she turned to Channel Seven, she stepped back and reviewed the scenes that popped up on the screen.

Soon the girls were standing next to her, observing the images of the outside of her townhouse. All that lived outdoors was still, seemingly asleep.

"The guys had a system like that," Wanda said, stepping back and pulling the bag that Clarissa had given her up against her chest.

"It's okay," Clarissa said. "I'm the only one who can see what's on the screen."

"What if they figured out a way to mess with your security camera?" Amber asked.

"Yes," Wanda said. "What if some dumb ass really is waiting to jump us outside? You said some utility guy was here yesterday, but he never even knocked on the damn door. How do you know he was legit?"

"Let me call security," Clarissa said. "The security company can confirm that there's no one outside and that no one has messed with the security system."

When Clarissa disconnected from speaking with the security company representative, she turned and told the girls, "Everything is okay. No one has been snooping around this morning. And," she added, "No one has done anything to the security system."

"What if they have and they did it in a way that the security company can't tell?" Trisha asked.

"It's okay," Clarissa said, placing her hands atop Trisha's shoulders. "It's okay," she repeated. "There's nothing wrong. And, besides, we have to go. We have flights to catch."

"Hold up," Wanda said. "Why are we leaving so much earlier than we said we would?"

"So we can get to the airport without hitting traffic," Clarissa lied.

Wanda pursed her lips.

Clarissa removed the chair from beneath the front doorknob. Then, she and the girls hurried to the Camry.

There wasn't so much as a stray cat out. Clarissa relaxed into the calm by pressing her back into the soft driver seat cushion as she drove further and further away from the safety of her home. Moments later, she punched the accelerator and sped down Interstate Four Hundred, churning up miles, bringing the girls closer to the Atlanta International Airport. Every few seconds, she glanced into the rearview mirror.

A semi pulled passed her and she put more foot weight on the accelerator. When she looked into the rearview mirror again, she spotted a van half a mile behind her. "Damn," she cursed beneath her breath. She had no idea who was driving the van. Yet, she convinced herself that she couldn't relax.

That's when an idea came to her. "Trisha," she said, handing her cell phone to Trisha who sat in the seat next to her. "Do a search on my phone and check and see if our flight is booked up, please."

"The flight's booked," Trisha said a moment later, looking at Clarissa's cell phone. "Why'd you ask? We already got our tickets, right?"

"Yes," Clarissa nodded. She glanced into the rearview mirror and saw that the van was still trailing them. "I just wanted to know about the flights," she added, taking the Camry from eighty to ninety miles an hour.

Half an hour later, when she pulled into the airport parking lot, she was relieved to see that the van was no longer behind them. Still, she told the girls to, "Grab your bags." Turning to Amber, she said, "Leave your bag in the car. We'll put it in the trunk. We have to hurry and get Wanda and Trisha home. Wanda's flight is first. After we get Wanda to her parents, we'll catch the flight to Indianapolis."

She released a deep breath when she didn't see the van circling the airport's large free parking lot. Only a few people peppering the lot, she and the girls ran from the Camry to the nearest airport shuttle. Their sneakers landed against the asphalt with a tapping noise. After they reached the shuttle, Clarissa prayed for the airport bus to show up within seconds. She prayed this although she didn't see the bus anywhere.

Next, she flipped her wrist and checked her watch. More than five minutes passed before the bus came around the corner. "Let's go," Clarissa told the girls, nearly pushing them onto the shuttle bus.

As she stepped onto the bus last, she spotted the white van out of the corners of her eyes. Her heart started racing as she wondered how long the van, its exterior yet dirty, ugly and hampered with dents that Clarissa hadn't seen before, had been near the shuttle stop. *"But, no,"* she thought. *"I stayed on the lookout for the van."* She shook her head, *"I didn't see the van once we got near the airport."*

She was quiet much of the shuttle ride to the airport. As hard as she tried not to, she worried to the point of anxiety about the van's whereabouts. Around her, the chatter of domestic and international travelers blended into a noisy swell. The bus was too crowded for her to walk to the back and look out the rear window to see if the van was following them.

That lack of knowledge left Clarissa with no choice except to turn to the girls and say, "As soon as we get off the bus, run toward the terminal. Stay together, but run."

The bus slowed to a stop in front of the Delta domestic terminal. Wanda clutched her bag, stood and giving out a chorus of "excuse mes" exited the bus first. Trisha, Amber and Clarissa were close on her heels. They ran toward the terminal's sliding entrance doors.

Staying several feet behind the girls, Clarissa kept turning and looking over her shoulder, staring through throngs of travelers for the guys she'd ran into at the Sandy Springs truck stop.

"Let's use the electronic check-in device to get our boarding passes," Clarissa said, jogging toward a vacant silver check-in machine.

Wanda's boarding pass printed, Clarissa keyed in details to print Trisha's boarding pass. Just as Trisha's boarding pass spit out of the machine, Clarissa saw three men, their faces mirroring the men's from the Flatgrill.

Clarissa cursed as she pulled on the end of the pass, forcing it out of the machine. "Damn," she repeated. She hated that the men continued to shadow them, and she started to wonder if one of the girls had been paid for by a wealthy buyer. The thought turned her stomach and fueled her with a rising, bitter anger. She pushed the girls and told them to, "Sprint up the stairs."

Wanda stumbled up the first two steps behind the force of Clarissa's push. "Don't push me again," she barked at Clarissa. "Keep your damn hands off of me."

"Just get your ass up the steps," Clarissa snapped. No sooner had she spoken the words did guilt sting her conscience. "I apologize," she told Wanda. "But, we're in danger."

The apology wasn't enough for Wanda. She turned sharp on her heels and scowled at Clarissa. As she did, she caught sight of the men less than two hundred yards behind them on the ground floor heading for the stairs. Without a word, she turned and sprinted up the stairs.

At the top of the stairs stood an airport security guard; she stood with her hands clasped at the front of her waist. Her hair was pulled back into a thick, single cornrow. As relieved as Clarissa was to see the guard, her heart didn't stop racing until the girls and she stepped into the security line to get cleared through the checkpoint.

"Don't turn around," Clarissa told the girls. "We're being followed. Three guys are ten people behind us."

She looked at a red and black Atlanta Braves poster game ad when she saw the girls' bodies stiffen. Their rising fear sent a chill up her spine. She wanted to run, flee the airport, rid herself of the girls. She wanted to forget that she'd met the girls. She wanted to free herself of the trouble that their arrivals had brought her.

The line inched forward and Clarissa watched Wanda, Trisha and Amber move like stiff tin soldiers, their legs going up and down like they had steel instead of bone in them.

Peering over her shoulder, she saw that the men were still behind them. When they reached the TSA advanced imaging scanner, Wanda stumbled backward. At first, it was as if someone had pushed her. Then, Clarissa saw the exchange. It had occurred so fast. A man had hold of Wanda's forearm, clutching her like a handcuff.

As if it had merely been a reflex, Clarissa dug her fingernails into the man's hand, pushing down harder and harder, finally breaking skin and drawing blood. Next to her, Trisha and Amber kicked the man, while Wanda jerked and shook her arm, struggling to free herself.

"What's the problem?" a TSA guard shouted, looking from Wanda to Amber and Trisha then at Clarissa, the man and the two other guys who'd started to approach, but were now pulling back.

"These men are human traffickers--" Clarissa yelled, glancing from the TSA guard to the other travelers in line.

Suddenly it was as if the men were merely ghosts Clarissa had imagined. When she turned, the men were gone. Heavy with disbelief, she craned her neck and looked down the checkpoint line. Desire to see the men, spot them in a crowd, started to overwhelm her. She turned in half circles, first to the left then to the right. Her wide sweeping searches yielded nothing. The men she had started to hate but was now desperate to see were nowhere to be found.

"We'll walk you to your flight," a TSA guard told Clarissa after the girls and she went through the image scanners.

"No," Clarissa said, shaking her head. "That won't be necessary. We're fine now. But, if you see those guys again, have them arrested."

The guard nodded, knowing that he didn't have evidence to contact law enforcement and have the men arrested. "Yes, Ma'am," he told her, happy to watch the scene dissolve in front of him.

It took three trips to the restroom, a visit to a boutique and a glass of water to calm Clarissa and the girls. They hung out in bookstores and crowded restaurants until they heard the Delta gate agent announce, "Flight 222 to Philadelphia is now boarding at Gate 23."

Wanda, Amber and Trisha were several steps ahead of Clarissa on the passenger boarding bridge when Clarissa turned and saw the men arguing with the gate agent. "You're not on the boarding roster--" she heard the agent relay to the trio, annoyance turning her voice edgy.

"--But, that woman's a kidnapper," one of the men screamed, pointing and waging his finger at Clarissa.

"We can check that out, but you don't have a ticket. You cannot board this flight. I'm going to have to ask you to step away from the gate."

The agent's words came like a gift to Clarissa. She let out a breath and resumed her walk across the bridge. Yet, with each step that she took a gnawing fear grew. "Dear God, please-please don't let those guys catch another flight to Philly. Please." Her prayer was barely ended when she was pelleted by a new fear. *"How did the guys get passed security?"*

Halfway into the flight, a dip then a hard bump that sent Clarissa crashing against Trisha's shoulder snatched Clarissa 's attention. The airplane, a Boeing 747, shook, jerking passengers forcibly from side to side. Wind thrusts shoved the plane, nearly turning it on its side.

"Ladies and gentlemen, please return to your seat and fasten your seat belt," the cabin manager announced. He continued, "Cabin crew, please be seated. We are entering an area of turbulence. Fasten your seat belt and remain seated until further notice. Thank you."

Clarissa peered through the small window in time to see how ominous the sky had become. When she went to look out the window again, Trisha lowered the window shade. Both Trisha and she leaned back in their seats, bracing themselves against the rising turbulence that rolled the 747 from side to side. When Clarissa peered at the passengers sitting in front of her, she saw their hands clutching their armrests.

A hush came over the passengers and the cabin crew. Combination of the rolling airplane, the eerie silence and her strong visual imagination created a tightness that developed into a firm knot at the pit of Clarissa's stomach. She closed her eyes and swallowed rising vomit. It burned in her throat.

The airplane jerked and Clarissa felt her stomach threaten to empty itself. She gripped the handrails and nearly bolted from her seat to run to the toilet. But, she steeled her nerves, tightened her grip on the armrests and sat as rigid as a wooden doll.

"Are you two okay?" she looked to the side and asked Wanda and Amber.

The airplane shook and Wanda landed against Amber's shoulder. When she did, a folded sheet of paper fell out of Amber's wallet onto the aisle floor.

Clarissa spotted the paper at once. When Amber didn't reach for the paper, Clarissa leaned forward and retrieved the note. Yet, instead of handing the paper back to Amber, she pulled it toward her chest. Glancing at Trisha, she saw Trisha holding an airplane magazine. "Probably trying to calm her nerves," Clarissa mused before she glanced at Amber and Wanda. Then, she unfolded the paper with slow precision, her fingers going over the top edge then back, turning the paper down. She stared at a man's name. Beneath the man's name was a telephone number. As much as Clarissa longed to dial the telephone number, she didn't. But, she couldn't rid herself of the urge to walk to the back of the airplane, enter the bathroom and call the man. Despite the fact that she didn't want to consider it, she couldn't stop herself from wondering if the man was one of the guys who'd been following them in the van.

She had to face it, really face it. She didn't know the girls. They were strangers. She did believe that they had been part of a sex slave trafficking ring. What she didn't know was how they really got into the ring. It pained her, but she couldn't confirm that none of the girls knew any of the guys prior to the kidnappings.

Guilt weighed on her but didn't stop her from refolding the note and burying it in her palm. She turned toward Trisha and said, "I'll be right back." Then, she grabbed her book bag, stood and walked to the back of the airplane.

"Ma'am," a cabin crew member called to her from where she sat at the back of the plane, right across from the bathroom.

"I can't hold it," Clarissa begged, "I'll pee all over myself if I don't get in there now," she added, leaning her head toward the bathroom door.

"Okay," the crew member acquiesced, lowering her voice. "But, get right back to your seat and stay there until we advise otherwise. It's for your safety."

"I understand," Clarissa said. Pulling the bathroom door latch, she entered the small space. The bathroom became like a hiding place. She sat on the toilet, pulled an envelope out of her book bag, and taking a pen out of a pocket at the front of her book bag, she wrote the man's name and telephone number on the back of the envelope.

She leaned forward on the toilet when she heard the cabin manager announce, "We have departed the turbulence zone. Passengers are permitted to get up to visit the lavatory. In a moment, we will turn the fasten seat belt light off at which time all passengers will be permitted to turn on WiFi devices and unlock their seat belt. Thank you. Enjoy the remainder of the flight."

A jiggle to the bathroom door startled Clarissa. Her hand went to her chest when she opened the door and saw Amber standing on the other side.

Clarissa moved her hands behind her back, again concealing the note in her palm. "I was just leaving," she told Amber. She moved the paper to her side while she inched beyond Amber.

"Some flight, huh?" Amber said, entering the bathroom.

"Yeah. I really had to go," Clarissa responded, glancing at the cabin crew member, the woman's brow tight.

When Clarissa reached her seat, she stumbled with intent and dropped the note back inside Amber's wallet, but not before glancing at Wanda who was talking with a passenger in the seat in front of hers. Then, Clarissa returned to her seat next to Trisha, who was looking out of the airplane window watching clouds go by.

"It's one of the reasons why I like to fly," Clarissa said, leaning close to Trisha so that she too could watch the clouds float.

"I've flown less than a dozen times," Trisha said, still looking out the window. "Hard to believe the sky was so dark just a little while ago. Now," Trisha smiled. "It looks like a clear spring day."

"I always thought that flying would be as nerve wrecking as this flight was a few minutes ago," Clarissa chuckled. "That's why I never wanted to do it before I joined the Navy."

"This was one bumpy flight for a minute," Trisha said, looking at Clarissa. "It was scary," she laughed. "All I wanted to do was get off this plane."

"With you on that," Clarissa said, biting back the urge to ask Trisha if she knew the man whose name was on the paper in Amber's wallet. The longer that she delayed asking Trisha, the more she started feeling like she was drifting away from the girls, building distrust in them for what might turn out to be nothing.

She exchanged chit chat with Trisha the remainder of the flight. As if mirroring what the sky outside the window had become, the airplane landed smoothly. After they were cleared to exit the plane, Clarissa stood and clutched her book bag.

"Did you call your parents?" she asked Wanda, as they walked side-by-side down the passenger boarding bridge to the baggage claim.

"They said they'll be inside the baggage claim area," Wanda answered.

Less than one hundred feet from the baggage claim area that was decorated with big green plants growing in large bright red ceramic pots, Clarissa spotted a tall, narrow woman, a black fedora hat pushed down on her head. Beside the woman was an even taller, stocky brown skinned man wearing a Philadelphia 76ers hat. Even from where she stood, Clarissa saw the man's hands tremble with nervousness. It was as if he was reaching for something, like he wanted to hold someone. Soon the man was running. The woman followed him, making haste on a limp, right leg. The man and woman raced toward Wanda, Clarissa, Amber and Trisha. The couple ran with their arms straight out. The woman's body shook as she ran, crying out, "Wanda. Wanda."

Wanda ran toward her parents with reckless abandon. The plastic bag that she carried flapped back and forth, hitting her stomach then her hip. "Mama. Daddy," she cried, her brazen demeanor crumbling into childlike dependency.

Tears streamed down her parents' faces. Their weeping grew loud. Soon, Wanda was sobbing in their embrace. Their voices sounded like a chorus of longing and regret mixed with joy and relief.

Clarissa stood alongside Amber and Trisha watching it all happen. Before she knew it, she found herself choking back tears. Wanda had been with her for less than three days, and already she was missing her.

She told herself not to, but she started to wonder if she would see Wanda again. That's when she started digging through her book bag for her business card, the card with freelance writer / novelist printed across its front.

Across from her, Wanda fell against her parents' chests. She and her mother clung to each other, rocking inside one another's arms, tears falling faster.

"Are you okay?" Wanda's mother stepped back and asked. She looked her daughter up and down, scanning her for the slightest bruise or injury.

"I'm fine physically," Wanda told her mother and father. "But, I'm gonna need help. My head's kinda messed up right now."

"We'll get you help," her father assured her, kissing her forehead.

"Mom. Dad," Wanda said, following her parents' gazes and looking across her shoulder at Trisha and Amber. "These are my amigas," she smiled. "Trisha and Amber were with me in those shit holes."

She stepped away from her parents and embraced Trisha and Amber. "I love you." Tears started to roll down her face again. "I'm going to miss you so much. I wish we had met some other way," she blubbered. "But, I'm going to miss you."

"We're going to miss you too," Trisha and Amber cried, squeezing Wanda's shoulders.

"You all can keep in touch," Wanda's mother said, a smile lighting upon her face.

"Yes," Wanda's father added. "Just exchange telephone numbers. You know how you all stay glued to your cell phones," he laughed.

"The men took our cell phones after they nabbed us," Wanda said. She looked at Amber and Trisha. Then, she glanced at Clarissa who she was surprised to find staring at a man on the other side of the floor.

"Clarissa helped us get these flip phones from Walmart," she told her parents.

Wanda followed Clarissa's gaze again.

"Everything all right?" Wanda's father asked Clarissa, now following her fixed look and staring at the man too.

"That guy looks familiar," Clarissa said.

"He's not one of the guy's," Wanda assured.

"No. No," Clarissa said. "I think I saw him while I was out jogging the day that I first saw Trisha." Pausing, she continued, "But, I'm not sure."

Everyone stared at the man. Feeling their unwelcomed attention upon him, the man walked off, moving toward the airport exit doors.

"Want me to go talk with him?" Wanda's father asked.

"No," Clarissa said. "We'll be fine in the airport."

"I could scare him off," Wanda's father offered. "It'd be more than my pleasure."

"Tell you what," Clarissa said. "Let's walk outside and see if we see him."

Moments later, Clarissa said, "There he is," as she pointed across the street to a rented SUV. "He's over there with those other two guys."

Wanda's father followed Clarissa's finger. "I see them."

"They don't see us though. I can tell by the lackluster way they're standing, looking right at each other, not canvassing the area."

"I'll get the plates and call them in to a friend," Wanda's father told her. "We'll know who the SUV is registered to in less than ten minutes. But," he raised a finger and said. "Those guys probably didn't use their real names or real ID to rent the SUV." After a pause, he said, "Let's go back inside."

"Fake IDs or not," Clarissa said, "They might not be involved in human trafficking. I'm getting to where I'm suspecting everybody now. I don't want to do that."

"It never hurts to be careful, especially in the type of situation you're in," Wanda's father told her.

Clarissa met his glance, then quickly turned away. Her growing suspicions pointed at so many people. As much as she didn't want to, she felt herself start to second guess her decisions.

"Thank you for taking Wanda and the other girls in," Wanda's father told Clarissa when they reached Wanda, her mother, Trisha and Amber.

"Yes. Thank you," Wanda's mother told Clarissa. "And, come here," she said, her arms open, creating enough space for Clarissa to easily fit inside.

While Clarissa and his wife embraced, Wanda's father walked to the second exit and snapped digital photos of the SUV. He also took pictures of the vehicle's license plate. It surprised him when the three guys didn't look up or seem to notice him.

"To give you all time to say good-bye, what do you say we grab something to drink from a cafe? I saw one close to here when your mom and I were walking to the baggage claim," Wanda's father said.

"Sounds like a plan," Wanda said. "You all cool with that?" She asked, looking at her mother, Clarissa, Trisha then Amber.

With a series of nods, they sealed the agreement and started walking to the nearby cafe. Half an hour later, when they stood to exit the cafe, Wanda's father pulled Clarissa to the side and told her, "The SUV is a rental. Two of those guys are from London. One of the guys is from Los Angeles. At least that's what their fake IDs show. Based on their fake IDs, they don't have plane tickets," he told her. "I checked."

"Good," Clarissa exhaled. "And, thank you." Seconds later, she said, "We best get going. We have another flight to catch."

"Thank you for taking care of our baby girl," Wanda's mother told Clarissa, hugging her tight.

"Yes. Thank you," Wanda's father smiled. His jaw quaked as he told Clarissa, "Be careful after you land in

Indianapolis. Call us if you need help. I mean that," he added.

"I will," Clarissa said. Then, she walked toward Wanda. They gave each other a hard look before they opened their arms and embraced. "Take care of yourself," Clarissa waved to Wanda, stepping outside her embrace.

"Thank you for everything," Wanda told Clarissa. "I know I wasn't always dope, but thanks. Thanks for everything. I mean it."

"Bye, Wanda," Amber and Trisha said, hugging Wanda one-by-one in a full circle. "We'll visit soon."

"Promise?" Wanda smiled.

"Promise," Amber and Trisha chorused.

They stepped toward each other and embraced again, hugging tightly, not wanting to let go. "See ya, Amber. See ya, Trisha," Wanda said, choking back tears. "I love you."

"We love you too," Amber and Trisha said, stepping away from Wanda and closer to Clarissa who had started to move away from the cafe toward the boarding area.

Hearing the Delta gate agent announce, "Flight 333 to Indianapolis is boarding at gate 25," fueled them forward. Still, they kept turning and looking over their shoulders at Wanda until she looked tiny, until they couldn't see her anymore despite how hard they tried.

The flight to Indianapolis was smooth, not a hint of turbulence. Before the airplane sped down the runway to land, Clarissa told Trisha to text her parents and remind them to meet her at the baggage claim area. They soon learned that there was no need for a text.

A red and white Indiana University baseball cap plopped down backwards on his head, Trisha's father was the first to see his daughter. He was standing at the end of the passenger boarding bridge, just outside the gate agent's desk. As soon as he spotted Trisha, he ran toward her, weaving in and out of passengers who were heading off the flight to the baggage claim.

Trisha's mother stayed near the bottom of the boarding bridge watching her husband's and daughter's reunion unfold as if she were merely a spectator in their lives. She held a small brown, beige and white Burberry handbag against her stomach. Right now, it was the only support that she had, her past mistakes haunting her, pinning her to the floor.

Trisha's father hugged Trisha so tightly, he lifted her feet off the ground. "Thank God you're okay," he told her. "It's such a blessing to have you home."

Her father held her hand while they walked down the bridge. It wasn't until they reached the bottom of the bridge that Trisha's mother stepped forward. "I'm so happy to see you, Sweetheart." She said, peppering Trisha's face with kisses.

"It's good to see you too, Mom," Trisha replied. She squeezed her mother's hand.

Clarissa watched the coolness between Trisha and her mother with unease. To escape the discomfort, she said, "You must be overwhelmed with emotion seeing each other for the first time in two years. You probably want to be alone to catch up." She paused, then added, "I hate to say good-bye, Trisha. But, we have to get going."

Another look at Trisha and Clarissa froze. She wanted to run, flee the rush of emotion that she felt rising within her. She couldn't stop thinking about the time that she'd seen Trisha hiding behind her Camry. Before she knew it, she was reaching out for Trisha, holding her, rocking her in her arms. A moment later, tears had started to wet her face when she let Trisha go. "Take care of yourself," she told Trisha, patting her on the back. "I'll always remember you fondly. Always," she nodded. "This can't stop you, Trisha," Clarissa added seconds later, the ends of Trisha's and her fingers touching. "You're going to live a very good life," she nodded then smiled at Trisha. "Watch," she smiled and nodded again.

"Thank you," Trisha said, stepping inside Clarissa's arms again. "Thank you for everything."

After Trisha kissed the side of Clarissa's face, she turned to Amber with outstretched arms. They hugged like they were blood sisters, pulling each other close, seesawing inside one another arms. After they separated, they held hands and promised to keep in touch.

"Where are you going next?" Trisha's father asked.

"Amber and I have to get back to Georgia."

"Will you be okay flying back?" Trisha's father wanted to know.

"Yes," Clarissa answered even as she worked to calm the growing knot at the pit of her stomach. She didn't know what it was. But, she had a nagging feeling that something wasn't right.

Chapter Sixteen

"It's a sunny eighty-three degrees in Atlanta," the pilot announced to the full cabin of four hundred and thirty passengers. "Take your seat and fasten your seatbelt. We'll be on the ground soon."

"We're almost there," Clarissa smiled at Amber. She took hold of Amber's hand. "This is such a blessing." Soon her smile faded into, "But, be very careful. This isn't the time for us to slip up."

"What about your friends?" Amber asked.

"I texted Gregory. He said that he'll meet us at the airport."

"Clarissa?" Amber asked, running her fingers across her wallet.

"Yes?"

"Are we really safe?"

The walk down the passenger boarding bridge into the Atlanta terminal was uneventful. Hundreds of people walked in front of and behind Amber and Clarissa, cocooning them in a sea of people.

In five to seven second intervals, Clarissa looked over her shoulder. Before she knew it, her breathing had become laborious.

Amber walked so close to Clarissa that Clarissa and her shoulders kept bumping.

"Stay confident," Clarissa said. "We cannot stand out. And, hey, Amber," she tried. "I want to ask you a question."

"Go ahead."

Lowering her voice to a whisper, Clarissa looked straight ahead and asked, "Did the guys put a price on you? I mean," she stammered, "did they sell you to someone?" She bit her lip as soon as she asked the question.

"I don't-don't know," Amber stuttered.

"Does the name Bill Walsh mean anything to you?"

"Where did you hear that name?"

"It came up when a friend ran a set of plates for a vehicle the guys were in," she lied.

"I don't know a Bill Walsh," Amber said, shaking her head.

"Okay," Clarissa said. She took one step away from Amber, fully aware that Bill Walsh was the name on the folded paper in Amber's wallet.

Their walk led them to the large terminal exit doors. Outside temperatures were balmy. The sky had a colorful haze. Winds blew gently, at times feeling still. Yet, instead of feeling hot, Clarissa felt embraced by the sun's heat. "Let me call Gregory," she told Amber.

She walked a few feet away from Amber, toward the glass terminal pane, so she wouldn't have to compete to hear over passengers' voices. While she walked, she filled Gregory in on Wanda's and Trisha's reunions with their families.

A warm feeling, as gentle as the day's summer heat, draped her when she ended Gregory and her call. If trouble was a long road, she felt like she was looking at the end of that grim path. She was starting to realize that the girls' homecomings were a returning to home for her too.

Absent warning and without so much as a bump or a verbal threat, her attention diverted. Suddenly, she was frantic, turning and calling out, "Amber." In another instant, she was shouting. "Amber. Amber. Amber." She ran one hundred yards one way down the sidewalk in front of the terminal. Then, she turned and ran in the other direction down the sidewalk.

Finally, she stopped by the outside baggage check-in booth and asked the man at the booth, "Will you please call Security for me? Hurry," she told him. "My daughter is missing."

The man snatched a black receiver out of its cradle and rang Security.

At the same time, Clarissa pressed one finger against her ear, reducing background noise while she spoke with Gregory. "Where are you?" she asked him, fear causing her hands to tremble.

"Just pulled into the parking lot," Gregory told her.

"They took Amber," Clarissa blurted. "She was standing right next to me. The next second, she was gone." She exhaled. "I asked the guy outside the baggage check-in to call Security. "

"Airport Security?" Gregory asked.

"Yes."

"You shouldn't have done that," Gregory told her. "That dude working the desk might not know how to handle this type of situation."

"Shit," Clarissa groaned, stepping away from the baggage check-in booth. A second later, she told the guy at the booth. "That's okay. I don't need Security after all." She shook her head. "I think I see my daughter."

She hurried away from the booth, her phone pressed against her ear. "I'm going back inside the terminal," she whispered to Gregory.

"No," Gregory told her. "Head for the exit booth across the street from the terminal." He paused. "Those dudes are probably parked outside the terminal. It's so they can grab girls and get away fast without being detected." After another pause, he added, "Do you have Amber's phone number?"

"Yes," Clarissa told him. "I have all of the girls' phone numbers. But, I hadn't thought about calling Amber. Are you sure it's okay? I don't want the guys to know that we're on to them. I don't want them to panic and flee the area. I can't lose Amber. We've come too far. I've got to get her home. Plus, she had the number for a guy named Bill Walsh in her wallet. I asked her if she knew a Bill Walsh and she said - no. She doesn't know I saw the name and number in her wallet. Wanda's father ran plates for a SUV some guys who looked to be following us rented and the name Bill Walsh came up."

"Could be a guy in the ring who was nice to her. She might have trusted him." He paused. "She might be naive."

"Yeah."

"We can't focus on that right now. We have to find her." Gregory spoke fast. "Call her and get across the street to the exit. Stand by the ticket booth and search inside every vehicle that you see. Whoever's working the ticket booth should be able to be trusted, if you need help. I'm on my way," he added. "Just parked." A second later, he said, "I see you. But, don't worry about me. Head for the ticket booth. I'll search the parking lot."

"My car is parked in the overnight economy parking lot," she told him.

"Doesn't matter right now," Gregory said. "Just get to the ticket booth."

"Okay," Clarissa said, hanging up her phone and sprinting toward the ticket booth.

"Please help me," Clarissa said, her words coming out raspy, full of breath, as soon as she reached the first ticket booth. "I need to find someone. Can you help me?" she asked, searching the fortyish woman's tan face. She was so focused on vehicles that passed through the gate that she scarcely noticed the gray streaks in the woman's short afro.

"Did you walk here?" the woman asked.

"No. My car is parked in the economy parking lot. Someone grabbed my daughter while we were leaving the baggage claim."

"Did you call the police?"

"Please help me," Clarissa begged, her hands coiled into half fists, not because she was angry, but because she felt a growing fear. Her eyes were wide, hungry for information. "Are there cameras at all of the terminal's exit and entrance doors?"

"You need to speak with Security," the woman told her. Then, looking over Clarissa's shoulder, the woman took a parking ticket from a driver.

Clarissa stepped to the side, but not before she examined the insides of the car. She stood at the side of the ticket booth inspecting each car that passed. Every few minutes, she hurried to the second ticket booth and looked inside vehicles that moved through that line exiting the airport.

In between checking vehicles, she called Amber. The phone rang twice before a voice crossed the line. She was shocked when she heard Amber's voice. "Amber,"

Clarissa said. "Are you safe? Where are you? Are you alone? Is someone with you?"

"They're watching me. They've been following us the whole time," Amber whispered. "While you were on the phone when we first came outside the terminal, one of them covered my mouth and another led me away from you. I tried, but I couldn't scream."

"You're not safe," Clarissa said, needing no further evidence that Amber was in imminent danger. "Where are you? Can you tell me that?"

"Looks like we're near the back of the airport," Amber whispered. "The guys are several steps ahead of me. With other people around to muffle sound and me whispering, I don't think they can hear me. Plus, you're not around. So, I think they think no one is going to come for me," she stammered. "At least not yet."

"Look at the walls. Is there anything hanging on the walls?"

"There's a large grey and white Crammer Hotel ad on the right side of the wall. We're close enough to the back of the hotel for me to see rows of airplanes. And, there's a small restaurant named Mitchell's less than twenty feet from where we are. Hurry," she begged Clarissa. "If you don't get here soon, I could end up right back in the same situation that I just escaped from a few days ago or worse."

"Okay," Clarissa said. "Hold yourself together. We're on the way. And, now you have my number in your phone. Text me when it's safe," she said. "And mute your phone, so the guys can't hear it ring."

"I already did that," Amber said. "They don't even know I have a phone. Hurry."

"I will." When Clarissa looked up, she saw Gregory running across the street in her direction. His yellow and black Tiger Asics hit the ground with a light touch. The back of his t-shirt flapped in the wind, pushing off his back then layering it again.

"I know where she is," Clarissa told Gregory. "We have to hurry."

"Did she tell you how many guys are with her?"

"Damn," Clarissa cursed. "Forgot to ask." She bit her lip when no one answered when she called Amber back.

Not to be defeated, she called Amber again. This time, Amber picked up. "I can't talk long."

"Okay," Clarissa said. "I'll be fast. Just tell me how many guys are with you and are you still in the area that you were in before?"

"There are two guys," Amber whispered. "And, yes, I'm in the same area. Hurry," she begged. "Hurry."

"We're on our way."

Turning to Gregory, Clarissa said, "There are two guys with her. They're near the back of the airport. I say we hop on a cart."

"I'm with you on that," Gregory said.

They ran inside the terminal, dodging three toddlers who played with character toys on the floor close to their parents' legs. Then, they ran down the long, shiny corridor, past two escalators, an ATM machine and an information booth.

"Start limping," Gregory told Clarissa the instant that he spotted an airport employee driving a cart outside a Mediterranean restaurant.

As if she'd been born crippled, Clarissa favored her right side. Her leg went down, her knee out farther than normal then slowly back up again. Her hips looked uneven, as if they hadn't been meant to work together.

Gregory waved at the cart driver, an olive skinned man sporting a pair of navy blue pants, a white shirt, grey airport vest, an undercut ponytail and a cross tattoo on the side of his neck. As soon as the man saw Gregory's hand swaying back and forth and Clarissa's hard limp, he slowed the cart to a stop. "Hop on," he said. "Where are you two headed?"

"To Mitchell's Restaurant," Clarissa directed. "We're meeting clients there. Important business meeting and we're late. Can you hurry?"

"You got it," the man said, pressing the cart pedal. "Can't go too fast though. There are a lot of people in here."

While they maneuvered around hundreds of people walking through the concourse, Gregory dug his iPhone twelve out of his pant pocket and called Paul and Carter.

His iPhone again in his pant pocket, he told Clarissa, "Paul and Carter are on the way."

Moments later, Clarissa told the cart driver, "You can stop here."

"But, we're not at the restaurant yet," the driver said.

"I've got to pick something up first," Clarissa lied.

With that, the man pressed the brake, smiled and thanked Clarissa for her five dollar tip and watched Gregory and her climb off the cart.

"She's over there," Clarissa leaned toward Gregory and whispered after they got off the cart just outside the Peppery Cafe. "And, those guys look familiar," she said, nodding toward two men who stood across the corridor at the edge of Mitchell's Restaurant drinking beer.

"They're waiting on someone," Gregory said, eyeballing the guys.

"What?"

"They might have found a buyer for Amber already."

"Damn," Clarissa grimaced. "That's why I thought they were so intent on finding us. They probably sold her a long time ago. Why else would they have kept following us?"

"Yeah," Gregory said. "I knew something was up when you said the guys were still here with Amber." He paused. "It's why I asked Paul and Carter to get here. She's not even a human to them. She's an investment. She's just money to them."

Clarissa kept her gaze glued on Amber. "Should I try to alert Amber that we're nearby?"

Gregory craned his neck and peered around the corner at the men. "Wait until she gets further away from those guys."

Charm bent in their direction and the guys turned away from Amber and started flirting with a waitress. That's when Gregory tapped Clarissa's forearm. "Text Amber now."

Clarissa prayed not to drop her phone, her hands trembled so badly. "Don't turn. Don't move," she texted Amber. "Gregory and I are less than twenty yards from you. Do-not-turn-around. When I tell you, start moving away from the guys. Tell them that you have to go to the bathroom. But, wait until I tell you."

"OK," Amber texted back.

No longer texting, Clarissa closed her eyes and let out a deep breath. "Gregory, let me know when to tell Amber to ask the guys to let her go to the bathroom."

"Okay. Let me call Paul and Carter. Keep an eye on Amber. I'm going over by the bar right next to this cafe and call Carter and Paul."

"Why do you have to go by the bar to call them--" Clarissa began. When she looked up, Gregory was gone.

Her tongue caught in her throat when she stood from her seat and didn't see Gregory. Although the Peppery Cafe was one corridor over from Mitchell's, Clarissa turned her back toward the corridor, desperate to avoid being seen by the guys keeping watch over Amber. She started moving down the corridor, away from Amber and the men. Seconds later, she recalled Gregory's instructions and retraced her steps, hurrying back to the Peppery Cafe.

The Peppery Cafe was within arm's reach when Clarissa heard footsteps. She turned and saw Gregory, Carter and Paul running down the corridor.

"Go in the bathroom around the corner from the cafe and text Amber. Tell her to meet you in the bathroom," Gregory told Clarissa.

Even as Gregory spoke, Paul and Carter took position, Carter at the front of the Peppery Cafe and Paul at the middle of the cafe, near the cash register. He stood with his back to Mitchell's.

Gregory stayed near the back of the cafe, his gaze fixed on Mitchell's.

"Meet me in the women's bathroom that's right across the walkway from the Peppery Cafe," Clarissa texted Amber. Then, she eased her way inside the bathroom.

Without returning the text, Amber shoved her phone in her pant pocket and approached the taller of the two guys.

As Gregory watched the scene unfold, he nursed a glass of water, not wanting to attract suspicion. He stood up when he saw Amber head toward the women's bathroom. His hope betrayed him as he heard one of the guy's say, "Hurry. Be back here in two minutes. We've got to leave."

"We've got two minutes," Gregory texted Paul and Carter via their group text. "The buyer must be close. Stay sharp in case the guys have a sudden change of plans."

The women's bathroom door closed with a hush. As soon as it did, Clarissa stepped outside the last bathroom stall. She looked over Amber's shoulder, checking for on-comers. A smile lit across her face when she saw that Amber and she were the bathroom's only occupants.

Amber nearly ran toward Clarissa, approaching her as if she were an old friend. As distrusting as she'd been with Clarissa a day ago, it didn't escape her how Clarissa had again fulfilled the role of rescuer for her.

Pressing a finger to her lips, Clarissa told Amber, "When we leave, you're going to be on the other side of me, away from Mitchell's. Just follow me. You're not going back with those guys. Gregory, Carter and Paul will handle them."

Amber nodded nervously, her eyes wide with fear.

"Do you have to go to the bathroom?"

"No."

"All right," Clarissa said. "Let me call Gregory and then we're getting out of here."

"Okay," Amber nodded in short, jerky motions. She shifted her attention to the long sink backsplash in an attempt to calm tremors that had started to shake her shoulders and hands.

"Here. Put this on," Clarissa said, pulling a familiar Panama roll hat out of her book bag. "Pull it all the way down over your head." She put her cell phone away and told Amber, "When we leave the bathroom, walk away from the wall. Don't respond to anyone calling your name." A thought presented itself. "What name do the guys know you by?"

"Amber."

"Just one more question." Hoping to assuage the guilt that stung her conscience, Clarissa peered at the floor. Then, wanting an answer more than she wanted to protect Amber's emotions, she looked up and asked, "Who is Bill Walsh?"

Amber didn't hesitate. "I thought I could trust him. He said he would help me."

"Is he one of the guys by Mitchell's?"

"No," Amber shook her head and revealed. "He's not here. Bill has a hairy mole below his left eye. He was one of the guys who met us on the road when we worked truck stops, hotels and when we worked out of rented houses in the suburbs. He was always there."

"Okay," Clarissa said, eager to know why Amber hadn't come clean about Bill Walsh while they were on the flight to Philadelphia. "Come here," she told Amber, opening her arms. "I love you." She stepped back, her arms fully extended, her hands resting on Amber's shoulders. "I really do. Not sure how we got separated before. We can't let that happen again. Walk away from the wall the entire time. Don't turn around. Just keep walking. I'll shield you."

Clarissa removed her hands from Amber's shoulders when she heard the bathroom door swing open. Amber and she watched two women, expensive Fendi handbags hoisted over their shoulders, enter the bathroom

"Keep your head up," Clarissa coached Amber as they exited the bathroom and made their way down the corridor. For the next request, Clarissa used a firm, stiff voice. It came like a reflex, in response to Amber's sudden attention shift. "Stop looking toward Mitchell's."

Regarding her captors more than Clarissa, a woman who'd proven herself a friend, Amber refocused her attention on Mitchell's. She even raised up on her toes so that she could see over the tops of the heads of a group of tourists and keep watch on her captors, both men still nursing a beer.

"Don't look over there," Clarissa whispered through clenched teeth. It wasn't until she pulled on Amber's wrist that Amber faced forward and looked blankly at the backs of the throngs of travelers walking toward the exit ahead of her. Her interest in the surrounding travelers didn't grow until she peered toward the opposite corridor, at people walking toward Mitchell's. A medium height, ebony skinned woman with a thick cornrow snaking down her back met Amber's glance. Shape of the woman's concave nose, her coffee brown oval eyes and her square chin mirrored Amber's. Excepting for the woman's Madewell jeans, split-neck blouse and flat form sandals, Amber felt like she was looking at her twin. Before she knew it, she was turning and looking toward Mitchell's. She didn't see the guys, not until she almost turned completely around. That's when she spotted them at the top of the corridor. One guy looked in her direction. He squinted, as if trying to make out her features from so far away.

"Turn around," Clarissa argued, grabbing and jerking Amber's wrist.

Amber was still looking at the top of the corridor, matching her captor's glance, when Clarissa tapped three fingers against her chest as Amber and she walked by the Peppery Cafe.

Gregory gave Clarissa a nod, then Carter, Paul and he stepped away from the cafe.

"Turn around and breathe," Clarissa told Amber. "I know it's scary, but you can breathe." Even as she spoke the words, Clarissa glanced over her shoulder. She almost smiled when she saw six more women entering the bathroom. Turning her head further to the right, she saw Amber's captors walking toward the women's bathroom.

"Let's pick up the pace," Clarissa told Amber. "We're going to Gregory's car. He handed me an extra set of his car keys when we met up earlier."

Terror demanding her attention, creating a strong impulse in her, Amber looked back. She nearly collapsed to the floor when she saw her captors at the edge of the woman's bathroom. "He didn't see me. He didn't see me. He looked right at me, but he didn't see me," she whispered as she rubbed her hand back and forth across her forehead. "They don't know where I am," she continued. "I hope they don't think that other woman is me and grab her." Under fear's dreadful grip, her legs functioned like rubber, making it hard for her to stay balanced. When she took another step, she leaned into Clarissa and, wiping the woman who looked so much like her from her thoughts, she nearly fell when she opened her stride. She kept glancing at Clarissa, concern drawing her face down. Her pupils were dilated, fixed with fear, as if they had been painted over her eye scelera.

"You're going home today," Clarissa said. "Today," she repeated. "Let's get to Gregory's car."

This time, when Clarissa looked over her shoulder, the Peppery Cafe was a blur. After they reached the end of the corridor, they hurried down two flights of steps. Then, Clarissa said, "Let's run."

They hurried outside and ran all the way to the hourly parking lot a quarter mile from the terminal. Clarissa punched the key alarm and they ran zigzag through the lot until they found Gregory's car, the vehicle's lights flashing. Fearing that they'd been followed, Clarissa fumbled with the key. "Damn it," she swore the second time the key slipped out of her hand

and fell to the ground. She unlocked the passenger door first, then she raced around the front of the car to the driver side. She wasn't halfway on the driver seat when her phone rang.

"Pull to the front of Express Airlines," Gregory said.

"Doing that now," Clarissa told him, sliding across the driver seat, turning on the engine and backing out of the parking lot. She sped toward the exit. After she paid the fare, she pointed the car toward Express Airlines.

Express Airlines in sight, Clarissa searched for a place to park. Before she could turn the car sharply toward the nearest open spot, she heard a deafening noise. It sounded like an eighteen-wheeler truck was backfiring, creating loud "pop, pop, pop" sounds.

She tightened her grip on the steering wheel when she saw Amber's two captors chasing Gregory, their guns pointing at Gregory's head. Her hand was on the door handle when she spotted Carter and Paul sprinting out of the Express Airlines terminal.

Onlookers stared at the unfolding scene. Some people froze and stood in the middle of the street, gawking as Gregory ran for cover. Other travelers screamed and sought shelter inside the terminal.

Gregory raced around the passenger side of his car as Carter and Paul closed the gap on the guys chasing him.

Without prompting, Amber opened the passenger door to let Gregory in. But, rather than climb inside, Gregory took his foot and slammed the door closed.

Carter kneeled behind the rear bumper of Gregory's car. Then, he stood and popped one of the guy's chasing Gregory in the shoulder. He hit the guy two more times, once in the knee and again in the shoulder.

Paul ran from the back to the front of Gregory's car, his pistol pointed at the other guy. "Drop it," Paul ordered.

The guy took aim at Gregory, then pulled the trigger. He grazed the top of Gregory's shoulder.

Paul reciprocated by landing two bullets against the guy's collar bone. It took a third bullet to bring the guy to his knees.

Piercing screams from onlookers grew. Parents grabbed their children, shielded them beneath their shoulders and ran inside the terminal.

His lacerated shoulder burning and stinging, Gregory hobbled toward his car. Extending his hand, he signaled Clarissa to be still. "We have to wait for the cops. There's been shooting. We can't just leave now. Paul and Carter have the two guys. When the cops get here, they'll take over."

"Thought you said that some cops are in on this-"

"--They are," Gregory told her. "That's why I'm getting ready to make a few phone calls." He leaned against the side of his car and made a round of calls to his friends in the police force, standup guys who he knew he could trust.

Moments later, police sirens rang out. Their red, blue and white car lights flashed, filling the area with noise and blazing lights. A dozen cops leaped from their cars and surrounded the Express Airlines terminal.

"Wait here while I go and talk with the cops I know," Gregory told Clarissa.

"But, you've been shot," she told him.

"Don't worry about me," Gregory said. "It's a surface wound," thinking that he knew how badly he'd been injured.

It took a long time for Gregory to stop filling the cops in on what had happened and hobble back to his car.

"Amber, please get in the back seat," Clarissa said. Then, she leaned forward and told Gregory to, "Sit up here. I'm taking you straight to the hospital. I already called Joann."

"Okay," Gregory said, sitting back on the seat. "Joann and I have spent way too much time at the hospital this month." He paused and added, "There's just one change."

"What?" Clarissa asked, turning the car away from the curb.

"Paul and Carter are going to follow us in case anyone else decides to get froggy." He took in a deep breath and squinted against the pain shooting through his shoulder. "Now, let's get Amber home. I can go to the hospital after we get her home."

"Okay," Clarissa nodded, her hands tight around the steering wheel. "But, if you look like you're slipping out of consciousness, I'm flooring this car to the nearest hospital."

"Agreed," Gregory said, too weak to put up a fight.

Clarissa drove the Dodge Charger eight miles down the road when Gregory sat up. He stared into the side passenger window and peered at the white Ford

Mustang shadowing them. "Think we're being followed." He shot Clarissa a telling glance. "You know what to do."

Clarissa pulled into the nearest convenience store parking lot.

The white Ford Mustang followed them.

Then, she pulled out onto the main road only to turn into a flower shop parking lot. That's when, out of the corners of her eyes, she spotted what she thought were Paul's and Carter's cars in the distance, about a quarter mile behind the Mustang.

Yet, those cars were too far away for Clarissa to be certain that they were, indeed, Carter's and Paul's. On top of that, the Mustang continued to shadow the Charger, its engine revving, signaling the driver's growing threat.

"Hang on," Clarissa said. She sped up a long, steep hill, then turned the car a sharp right and sped down a two lane road. "I think we lost them," she announced when she saw no more than a squirrel run across the street as she looked into the rearview mirror. "Amber? Which way to your home from here?" She looked over the top of Amber's head, through the back windshield, for the Mustang.

"And, call your parents and tell them that we're on the way," Gregory advised.

Clarissa laid her hand on her chest. "Thank you, Lord," she said when she looked in the rearview mirror and saw Paul and Carter behind them. She craned her neck, but she didn't see the Mustang. "Not sure how we lost Paul and Carter before. But, now I see them about a quarter of a mile back."

After a series of turns which led them passed a 7-Eleven, a strip mall, a string of restaurants, a gas station and an elementary school, they pulled in front of a white and green three-story wood house. This time when Clarissa looked into the rearview mirror, she saw tears streaming down Amber's face.

"We're here," Clarissa said, parking the car and opening the door.

Carter and Paul parked their cars behind Gregory's.

A short woman with a medium build and a curly afro sprang from a padded porch lounge chair. A man standing with his stomach pressed against the house's front screen door pushed the door open and ran after the woman. They were soon joined by three girls and two boys ranging in age from six to fourteen. "Amber! Amber!" they screamed, rushing at Amber with such force that she fell back. Their arms went around Amber like she was gold. "My baby! My baby!" the short woman cried, tightening her grip on Amber, pulling her closer. She, her husband and the children held Amber, feeling her body shake beneath the weight of longing to never let them go, missing the time with them that her captors had stolen from her, time she'd never get back.

Clarissa, Gregory, Carter and Paul watched the family reunion from where they stood at the edge of the front lawn. Suspended between curiosity and relief, they turned to leave. As they did, Amber called out, "Come here."

"Mama and Dad, all of you," Amber announced, her voice a blend of sorrow, happiness and uncertainty. "This is Clarissa," she said, pulling Clarissa near her. "She helped save my life. She helped save Wanda and Amber too. They're two girls who were with me."

"Thank you," Amber's father told Clarissa, wrapping an arm around her.

When he stepped back, Amber's mother approached Clarissa. Dark streaks went down the sides of her face, tears having mixed with her mascara. "From the bottom of my heart," she began, looking into Clarissa's eyes, "Thank you," she cried. "I can't thank you enough."

Her tears gaining strength, she broke into an outright cry then fell against Clarissa's chest weeping.

"And, this is Gregory, Paul and Carter," Amber continued. "Without them, we wouldn't be here."

Amber's father approached Gregory, Paul and Carter with his hand extended. "Thank you, Man," he said to each of them as he shook their hands.

"She's going to need psychological support," Clarissa lowered her voice and told Amber's mother.

"Yes," Amber's mother agreed. "And, we're going to get her that help. But, first, we are going to celebrate Amber being home." Shaking her head, she added, "You don't know how hard I've been praying."

"I can't even imagine," Clarissa admitted.

"Come here," Amber's mother beckoned Gregory, Paul and Carter. She folded her arms over their backs and hugged them tightly. "Thank you," she stepped back and said, dabbing the corners of her eyes. Moments later, she, her husband, Amber and her siblings stood on the sidewalk at the front of their home waving to Clarissa, Gregory, Paul and Carter as they pulled their cars away from the curb.

Curling her hand, Clarissa tapped the horn twice. Yearning rose within her. She missed Amber, Wanda and

Trisha until her chest felt tight. The further away from Amber the car went, its new tires spinning absent sound, the harder the lump developed in her throat. She blinked fast, fighting back tears.

"We are going to the hospital," Gregory said, Clarissa and he now alone in the car. "But, first circle the block. I want to make sure that Mustang is nowhere near here."

The streets were serene. Except for four girls double dutching, there wasn't a soul outside. Then, Clarissa saw it, hard white metal in the distance. "Damn. There it is," she moaned after they drove one block over from Amber's home.

"Pull to the side of the car," Gregory told her. "Paul and Carter are pulling in front of the Mustang. Stay here," he told her as he took hold of his gun and opened the door.

Gregory, Paul and Carter were inches from the Mustang's doors when the driver bolted upright. Before he could put the Mustang in drive, Gregory and Paul pulled their guns. Realizing that the odds were against him, the guy fell back against the seat and put his hands on the steering wheel.

"Give me your gun," Gregory told the guy. While he took the gun, he ogled the mole just below the guy's left eye.

On the other side of the car, Carter called a cop friend. They stayed with the Mustang until the cop arrived.

"We can't arrest him," the cop told Gregory, Carter and Paul. He looked the guy over, ran his tags and checked his identification. "We don't have anything on him. His record is clean. What I will do is warn that lady named Amber you just told me about and her family to be on the lookout for this character. I'll instruct them to call the police if they see him within a mile of their home."

After the guy in the Mustang, who was followed by the cop, pulled off, Clarissa climbed behind the wheel of Gregory's car and texted Amber a picture of the guy and his tags. Then, she drove Gregory to the hospital.

A day later, she sat in her Sandy Springs townhouse chatting with her sister, April.

"Wish you had told me what was going on," April said. "I'm still trying to absorb what you told me last night. You have no idea how much I wish that I could have helped you. It scares me even now to think of all that you and those girls went through, sends a chill into my bones."

"I know," Clarissa nodded. "I know you would have come down here in a flash. But, I couldn't risk the girls' lives. I just couldn't do that," she repeated. Shaking her head, she said, "I'm so glad that they are all safe."

"Yes," April admitted. "That is what's important. Thanks for at least keeping in touch by sending me text messages. All said, I'm so very glad that you're okay. I cried last night after you told me what the girls and you had been through."

"Love you, Sis," Clarissa smiled. "This coming weekend, I'm flying to Ohio to hang out with you. I need to be with family after all this madness."

"Would love for you to come home," April said. "It'll also give me a reason to take a mini-vacation from work."

"Things still hectic at work?"

"Are you kidding?" April laughed. "Don't think the pace at work is going to slow down anytime soon."

"Thankfully, you have your kids and husband to keep you in balance," Clarissa shared.

"That's true," April said. A second later, she blurted, "Tell you what."

"What?"

"I'm predicting that in three years, you're going to meet a loving, confident man and start your own family."

"Yeah?" Clarissa laughed.

"Yeah," April smiled. "You'd make a great mother, not to mention how good of a woman you are. And, you definitely can hold your own, I don't care what you're facing. You've been that way since we were kids."

"That's sweet, you wishing a loving, romantic relationship for me," Clarissa said. "But, I'm going to fly solo for awhile longer, especially after what I just went through."

"Have you heard from any of the girls?"

"Yes," Clarissa beamed. "I spoke with each of them on the phone this morning." She paused. "They're all doing good, considering. And are they ever happy to be back with their families. Trisha emailed me a picture that she sketched of the girls, including Jackie Davis, and me. She made it look like we were all together in a big, happy group, like we were a family."

"Well, you moved to Georgia after you got out of the Navy because you love the outdoors, hiking and all so much. Knowing you, Georgia will be home for a couple more years before you take off for the next adventure. You always were a bit of an explorer. Just don't get too far out. This world can get crazy."

After Clarissa ended her conversation with April, she turned and looked through her living room window. Squirrels scurried up a tree. A neighbor's black and white cat sat in its dining room window watching finches, eastern phoebe and hummingbirds fly in front of the window.

A moment later, after she'd watched nature's playfulness, Clarissa started typing frantically on her laptop. Her fingers sped across the keyboard, hurrying to get the story down. Less than four hours later, she'd typed twenty pages on her new novel, a story that centered on four girls who'd escaped human trafficking, all four of them saved.

IMPORTANT NOTE/RESOURCES

Human trafficking is a real issue impacting the globe's human citizenry. As of 2020, there were an estimated 40.3 million victims trapped inside this web of modern slavery. Human trafficking takes place in suburban homes, hotels, apartments, etc. Below are resources and support for anyone trapped in this human trauma. If you or someone you know or suspect needs help, consider reaching out to one of the below sources. Within the United States, there are homes and hotlines that you can call. Other global help organizations are also below. You can also volunteer to help an organization. Whatever you do, please don't choose to sit back and be silent.

National Human Trafficking Hotline (United States) - 1 (888) 373-7888

National Human Trafficking -
https://humantraffickinghotline.org/

U.S. Department of Health & Human Services, Office on Trafficking in Persons -
https://www.acf.hhs.gov/otip/about/ways-endtrafficking

U. S. Department of State, Global Hotlines -
https://www.state.gov/human-trafficking-hotlines/

Polaris Project - https://polarisproject.org/

National Center for Missing & Exploited Children – http://www.missingkids.org // 1-800-843-5678

In the United States, January is National Slavery and Human Trafficking Prevention Month

Global Modern Slavery Directory (listing of organizations around the world that work to end human slavery and sex slave trafficking) – https://globalmodernslavery.org/

"And I am convinced that nothing can ever separate us from God's love." – Romans 8:38

****

"For whosoever shall call upon the name of the Lord shall be saved." – Romans 10:13

Read More Books by Denise Turney

Love Pour Over Me

Portia (Denise's 1st book)

Long Walk Up

Pathways To Tremendous Success

Rosetta The Talent Show Queen

Rosetta's Great Adventure

Design A Marvelous, Blessed Life

Spiral

Love Has Many Faces

Your Amazing Life

Awaken Blessings of Inner Love

Book Marketing That Drives Up Book Sales

Love As A Way Of Life

Escaping Toward Freedom

Visit Denise Turney online – www.chistell.com

Made in United States
North Haven, CT
23 May 2023